SEVEN TERRORS

SEVEN TERRORS

Selvedin Avdić

Translated from the original Bosnian by
Coral Petkovich

istrosbooks

English-language edition first published in 2012 by
Istros Books
London, United Kingdom
www.istrosbooks.com

© Selvedin Avdić, 2012
Translation © Coral Petkovich, 2012

Cover image courtesy of Guliver Image d.o.o. Zagreb
The cover design of this book is based on the original design for
Sedam strahova (Algoritam, Zagreb, 2009)

ISBN 978-1-908236-09-8

Typeset by Octavo Smith Ltd in Constantia 10/13

Printed in England by
Imprint Digital, Exeter, EX5 5HY

This project has been funded with support from the European Commission.
This publication reflects the views only of the author, and the Commission
cannot be held responsible for any use which may be made of the information
contained therein.

Education and Culture DG

Culture Programme

Whoever ends up reading this text will not be my choice, as I have no say in the matter. Maybe that's a good thing, because I've never managed to choose the best option in my life. So let chance decide and hope it doesn't bring me some insufferable cynic.

This story, which I wish to retell in the best possible way, begins on the seventh of March 2005. On that day, the daily newspaper *Liberation* published a photograph of a municipal worker cleaning an enormous pile of snow from some street in Sarajevo. In the same issue, on the fourth page, a photograph of the village of *Ljute na Treskavici* appeared. On the pale imprint of the photo the roofs of the houses emerged from the drifts of snow, and the heading informed us that the heaps were seven metres tall.

Almost the whole of winter passed between alternations of fog and rain. At the beginning of March, the snow began to fall as though it had gone mad. The flakes were small and round like balls of Styrofoam, but persistent; they were pouring down for days. The town children delighted in them for the first few days. They made slides on every slope in town, and sledges were scraping the streets until late at night. But soon they became bored, so that this March ought also to be remembered as the time when even snow succeeded in being tedious for the children. By the time the last sledges abandoned the streets, the snow was purely an inconvenience.

These things happened not long ago, so I can remember the details quite well. In fact, I shall endeavour to convey everything exactly, because that is, after all, in my own interest. Maybe I won't succeed in retelling precisely the exact words of certain conversations; that is understandable; but I shall try to reconstruct them as truly as possible. They are very valuable for the continuity of the story. And I shall be completely sincere; while lies are attractive, they are also too expensive. And I'm not quoting here, I am speaking from experience.

I shall start the story like this.

I had spent nine months in bed. I wasn't ill, I felt quite alright. Physically, at least. Or at least nothing worse than usual. It was simply that I could not find a strong enough reason to leave my bed. I would lie for hours on my back and watch the rays of sunlight coming through the holes in the blind. I listened to the gurgling of the water pipes, the muffled voices of my neighbours through the walls, the creaking of the mechanized lift, the claws of the pigeons scrabbling on the tin window sills. I stared at the ceiling, ate sweet biscuits dissolved in water... slept... and that was all. That was all I did during those days, and all I wanted to do. I was not happy. Later on I shall explain to you why not. For now, so that at the very beginning of the story I do not leave any parts unclear, I shall point out that after ten years of marriage, my wife, who I always thought could not imagine life without me, had left me. As there is no place for lies in this story, I shall admit straight away that her departure was entirely my own fault.

On the night between the sixth and the seventh of March, all at once and without any reason that I could understand, I decided it was time I left my bed. On Monday, the seventh of March, 2005, I returned amongst the living. I opened my eyes at the first sound of the alarm clock, exactly at seven o'clock. I washed myself, cleaned my teeth, and even did my morning gymnastics, four push-ups which made me dizzy in my head and nauseous in my stomach. Then I lit my first cigarette. Oscar Wilde, if I remember rightly, said that cigarettes were the torches of our self-confidence and that with their help we could withdraw into the sphere of private perception. Cigarettes are for me a bad habit, a drug which does not take hold and, maybe, a mild remedy offering peace of mind. Besides, I'm never alone with a cigarette, as the classic advertisement says.

With this company between my teeth, I set off on my first adventure. I suppose I don't have to explain that I was nervous, frightened, unsure. But, it was time for a change. I wrapped myself in my coat and went outside. I wanted to start the morning with newspapers, to read about what I had missed over the past nine months, how the world had been stirring around my bed. A light wind was twirling the little snowflakes in the air. Some of them fell behind the collar of my coat. They were not unpleasant. I grabbed the copy of *Liberation*, quickly, so that the saleswoman didn't have time to start a conversation, left my change and sneaked back to my flat. I put my coffee pot on the stove and turned the radio on. 'The Rolling Stones will be playing a song for you this morning. We'll be listening to 'Street Fighting Man', whose musical legacy was recorded long ago, in 1968.' The voice of the radio host was serious, almost moved to tears, as though she were reading a report about the death of someone important. That announcement awoke in me a long-absent sense of calm, an old-fashioned peace, a feeling of safety which smelt like childhood. Such a feeling had not visited me for a long time. I stretched and tried to breathe it in, to feel it in my nostrils, my lungs, to hold onto it so as to be able to remember it well.

I drank my coffee, listened to the musical legacy and watched through the window as people pushed their way through the snow, which had grown another three feet during the night. Above them, a flock of tame white pigeons was flying round and round. I opened the newspaper. At the top of the second page, I found an article saying that since 1995 the teams from the Federal Commission for the Search for Missing People had found 363 mass graves and from them exhumed 13,915 victims. On the fifth page, the Epidemiological Service of the Federal Institute for Public Health warned that bad weather increased

7

the risk of infectious diseases, especially capricious respiratory diseases, and meningococcal infections, but also others such as hepatitis, stomach typhus and dysentery. On the pages set apart for world news, Giuliana Sgrena, a journalist from the Italian newspaper *Il Manifesto*, described how she had been freed from prison in Iraq, and accused American soldiers of firing at her car. All of Italy, stated the *local* reporter from Rome, was mourning the late Nicola Calipari, an agent of the Italian Secret Service who had been killed by an American patrol. Vladimir Putin was preparing for the celebration of the Day of Victory over Fascism; Jacques Chirac promised that he would support Palestinian independence, and the boxer Mike Tyson, at the festival in San Remo, had sung a version of the song 'New York, New York'. The television program offered viewers the choice between three films – the action thriller *Once in a Lifetime*, the melodrama *And That's Love* and the biographical drama *Frida*.

While I was thinking about what kind of film would suit the first day of my return to life, I heard someone knocking on the door: three times, lightly. At first, I thought I had misheard, since it was a long time since anyone had knocked on my door, so early in the morning. But then came another three knocks, followed by the bell. I got up from the chair, went towards the door and then stopped abruptly. In the mirror, I came across a melancholy, crumpled and pale image. I was wearing misshapen trousers full of glistening, luxuriant spots and a jumper that had once, before the war, been green, with a big sign on the front denoting the Mahnjača factory. It crossed my mind that it would be a good idea to change my clothes; then decided that there had already been enough changes in my life for the first morning there.

Mirna stood in the doorway. Fresh and smiling. Behind me gaped my one-bedroom flat, like the mouth of a giant with bad teeth.

'Good morning. I'm not too early, am I?'

It was then that I remembered. I remembered that there had perhaps been one more reason for me getting out of bed that day. The night before, I had spoken to Mirna on the telephone. She had woken me up and I had been drowsy, so I couldn't recall what we'd been talking about. At the time, I'd only wanted to finish the conversation as soon as possible and to return to bed. But she must have said she wanted to see me, or something like that, because there she was, standing there in the doorway with a wide smile.

'It looks as though I haven't come at a good time.'

I hitched my trousers up on my hips, looked back around the room and answered:

'You know, actually you haven't. Please, can you come back in an hour?'

My voice was hoarse, squeaky and hollow, woken up from a long silence. But she understood, smiled again, nodded her head and went away down the staircase.

The hour which I had wheedled out of her was intended to give me time to spruce up the flat; despite not really believing that she'd return. I know that I wouldn't have done in her place; I wouldn't return if the person who was waiting for me looked, thought, behaved and, generally, lived as I did. Since that was what I truly believed, I went back to the chair and sat down. For, after all, I was not in the least bit happy at the time...

I tried to remember the telephone conversation with Mirna, but without success. I had known her superficially, in that time before the war, when I knew many people in that way. We had talked only a few times. She liked painting and I think that was what we mostly talked about, even thought I am far from being an expert on that topic. It must be that the people she had met knew even less, because she followed every comment or flimsy conclusion of mine with enthusiasm. Then, during the war, she just disappeared. I didn't even notice when she left because at that time everything was disappearing – people, habits, things, customs, a whole pile of words. The town itself changed, almost completely. I got used to people going away, somehow quite easily, just as I adopted as a normal occurrence the shortage of food, water, electricity. Just as Čoka liverwurst had disappeared from my life, in the same way I noticed that a friend who had used to enjoy it was missing too.

When the doorbell rang, I realised I was wrong: she had come back. Then I was sorry I hadn't at least pushed the old socks and dirty plates into a corner. But in front of the door stood Ekrem, the caretaker in the apartment building and a taxi driver out in the street. In his hand he held a large notebook, with the pages criss-crossed with tables of numbers.

'Up early, neighbour? Payment for the cleaning lady, you know we collect from the tenants on the seventh of every month. Since you are still among the living, you owe nine months.'

I turned around to get my wallet from the pocket of my coat, knowing full well that, during that time, Ekrem was craning his neck to look into the flat. He always did that, forcing housewives to be careful to clean up a bit before his visit. When I turned back again, he took a quick step backward, smiled and indicated with his chin towards his fat stomach.

'Pretty good jumper, eh neighbour?'

The woollen jumper, with a big stylised deer baying at the moon, was stretched across his stomach. I nodded my head.

'I earned it with my cock – he informed me with satisfaction.'

I knew that too. He was always bragging about how his ex-wife was still sending him presents from abroad, even though she was married to some German pensioner. What Ekrem was trying to explain was that she was buying him presents in gratitude for those wild nights and in honour of his phenomenal sexual expertise.

'How are you? Or is it better not to ask?'

I nodded my head again and gave him the money. He winked at me and held out the notebook for me to sign. I shut the door and heard him ringing the bell on the door across the way: 'Up early, neighbour...? Nice jumper, eh?'

At that point, I decided to tidy up the flat a bit, after all. Just in case Mirna came back. I didn't take too much care; I just put away those socks and plates. I didn't have the strength to do much else, so I went back to the chair and waited...

Outside, a man and a woman were playing with a little girl in the snow. The man shut his eyes with his hands, and the other two, giggling, looked for a hiding place. They found it in a small cave scooped out of the snow. The man opened his eyes, fell to his hands and knees and began to sniff their footprints. His big moustache was cleaning the snow in front of him. When their tracks led him to the hiding place, he barked loudly, made a forward somersault and rolled inside. After him, with much more creaking than necessary, a small snow-covered door shut. A flock of white pigeons circled above, faster and faster, until they became a shimmering disk. The disk formed into an arrow which for a short time was calm in the sky, then turned towards the earth and swooped down with a hiss. While the birds, like large darts, burst like machine-gun fire into the snow, the radio behind my back started playing a fanfare and the doorbell began to clamour. I smoothed down my hair and turned the handle.

In the doorway stood a man with big, blood-shot eyes: the biggest eyes I have ever seen in my life. He said something to me, but no matter how much I tried, I couldn't understand a word. His small mouth moved like earthworms in the mud as repeated what seemed to me to be the same words. I asked him to say it again, I told him I couldn't understand a thing, but he didn't listen. He seemed veiled by his huge eyes, which somehow prevented me from seeing the rest of his face. The dark pupils swam in blood and in their clear reflection, my frightened face lay suspended. His mouth moved faster and faster, it seemed that he even reached the point of shouting, but I couldn't know for sure... And then I woke up.

Darkness had already drawn long shadows in the snow by the time I opened my eyes. The clock showed that I had slept through the whole afternoon, which was nothing unusual. At that time I could sleep constantly. It was enough for me to sit down, to stretch out my legs and already my vision became cloudy. No matter how long I slept I was still always sleepy. But it was enough sleeping. I went to the bathroom with the firm decision to wash myself. Turning on the tap, I gazed into the stream of water. It was magnificent, shining, fresh. I could have looked at it for hours. In fact, I did.

Mirna didn't come back that day. I waited for her on the chair, gazing through the window. Snow was still falling, as though it wanted to stop the very life of the town. But it was not successful. People kept stubbornly trampling on it. They passed by in front of the window and made paths which crazily multiplied and crossed without any order at all. It was hard to find any space in the snow on which no-one had stamped. In order to find fresh snow you had to get up very early, before everyone else, otherwise there was no sense going out, for you could watch everything from the window. I succeeded in finding out which window was the first to light up in the neighbouring apartment block. Then I finished watching half a movie (I decided on the love story) and turned over a few pages of a book. I don't remember which one, but I do remember thinking that it was enough for the beginning of my return to life. And then I finally fell asleep.

The next day, around midday, I stood before the window with a big cup of coffee. On the radio a cook was explaining how to barbecue fish – 'for a thickness of three centimetres you need ten minutes' – or something like that. On the street, women were carrying bouquets of flowers. Every single woman had at least one and to me it seemed as if they were carrying them like a trophy or like a conductor's stick. Then the doorbell made its announcement and in front of the door stood Mirna, with an even bigger smile than yesterday.

'Today you have to let me in. After all, it's International Women's Day.'

Indeed, it was the eighth of March. She came inside, and suddenly I was completely unnerved. I recall feeling that I couldn't remember how to entertain a woman who had called by unexpectedly. I offered her a cup of coffee, but she refused and in so doing, deprived me of the one idea I'd had. I sat down on the chair and put my hands in my lap. But, even confused like that, I still enjoyed the sight of her sitting in my kitchen.

Maybe this is the right place to describe Mirna for you. It would be good if I could find some well-known woman with whom I could compare her, but I can't think of any such person. She has black hair, cut short, almost regulation Yugoslav National Army length. You could say she is short, a few kilograms overweight, with a large mouth which would perhaps look better on a bigger face. Her eyes are black, with a ball of light in the centre, and her smile is her best feature: sincere, warm and ready to reveal itself at the slightest provocation. Such a smile can be like a remedy. Her smile made Mirna a beautiful woman, yet she was still not more beautiful than my own wife. (I compare all women to my deserting wife. Just as religious fanatics see a prophet's face in every stain, I recognised my wife in every other woman.)

It has occurred to me how I can best describe Mirna: she was somehow pure, with precise lines of body and face, as though a photomontage had been placed in my kitchen. I don't how long I sat staring at her, but it seemed to me that she wasn't bothered by it. She didn't speak, she only smiled. Silence did not seem to worry her, whereas it drove me crazy. Yet still I did nothing to break it. In fact, I even sustained it; I started to observe the flat through her eyes and immediately came to the conclusion that she could not possibly like it. Dust covered everything; if the room could have been shaken up thoroughly, large pieces of fluff would have kicked up a storm like inside those little snow-domes. Not one object in the flat had any shine, all the colours were subdued, and even the morning light was not having any effect, as though the gloomy room was soaking it up. Yet I couldn't move the curtains apart, for I was afraid a stronger light would uncover much worse things. I got up from the chair, smiled feebly in lieu of an explanation and opened the window to at least get rid of the smell of tobacco, sweat and used up oxygen – the smell of loneliness. Then I thought that some music might help, recalling how it can easily change the atmosphere of any room. Do an experiment, if you don't believe me. In a completely empty room, play different types of music and you will see how the shadows shift, the air stirs, the nuances of light change, as the room adjusts itself to the music, like the scene changing from act to act in the theatre.[1] There is no such thing as complete silence. It does not exist. At least not in this world, maybe in outer space or in the bowels of the earth, where it's only cold and dark. I put a CD into the tray of the player. I can't remember which one.[2] I seem to remember the playing of slow trumpet music. That's what I put on when I am feeling nervous. And at that time, if I remember rightly, I was rather nervous.

Mirna waited patiently for me to finish my preparations. I went back to the table and all at once we began to talk, as though we had accidentally tuned into the right frequency. She talked about Sweden, their big wide libraries where the books are arranged like sculptures, she boasted how she too could walk around in winter weather with wet hair and not catch cold, and she told me a story about the most nervous animal in the world – the Yarva, which cannot tolerate another Yarva within a hundred square kilometres. I didn't say much; mainly I just threw in comments between her sentences about how different it was here now, compared to before the war, and at the same time, somehow the same; and yet, of course, very different from Sweden.

We talked for a long time like that, maybe two whole hours, and all the while I was waiting for the moment when she would finally mention the reason for her visit. It seemed to me that she consciously procrastinated and kept quickly trying to invent a new theme, just to fill up every last piece of silence. She told me how in Sweden she avoided people from our country, that they were divided into national clubs where they hugged one another to the sounds of turbo-folk, and fought against a background of nationalist patriotic songs.

Suddenly she asked me, 'Do you remember my father?'

Of course I remembered Aleksa, we were friends. I knew him much better than I knew her.

I nodded my head, and she asked me a new question, 'Did he drink a lot?'

Of course I remembered that Aleksa drank a lot more than he should have. Just before the war, when the disaster could already be foreseen, his thirst suddenly began to grow. In the beginning he tried to hide it. He would go to the kafana, hurriedly, in a business-like manner, greeting the guests with a small inclination of his head, and he would order a double brandy. As soon as the waitress put the glass on the table, as soon as it clinked on the wood, Aleksa would grab it, swallow the alcohol down his throat in one gulp, put the glass down on the bar with a ringing sound, and depart. This time without any greeting. All that in a few seconds: tick-tock-tack and outside. Afterwards we learned that he repeated the same ritual in a whole series of different kafanas.

As soon as he left the first, he went across the road to the next one, and then he went down the boulevard, went into the kafanas he found there, called in at the deserted hotel bar, and from there went over to the kafana at the bus station, then the little grill place where taxi drivers warmed themselves; from there to a few more cafes where at night techno music was buzzing, then to the Lovers of Small Animals Club, then the theatre bar, the pizza place, and the billiard club; he went down the main street, drank one more at the kiosk on the marketplace, and in the express-restaurant. After two hours, and having made a complete circle, he returned to the first kafana. He stood in the doorway, blowing on his hands to warm them, as though he wanted to give the impression that he had endured a hard working day. He greeted the waiters loudly and heartily ordered a double brandy, then sipped it slowly, already completely drunk. We quickly discovered what he was doing, but no-one let on. His manoeuvring to quench his monstrous thirst we called 'Aleksa's Brandy Circuit'. I didn't see him often during the war, but I doubt he was able to break such a strong habit.

I didn't tell her all that. I only mentioned that during the war there had not been enough alcohol for anyone to 'drink a lot'.

'Aleksa just drank a bit, on occasion, like all of us...'

That is exactly what I said to her. I thought an answer like that would please her, but it did not. Her nostrils quivered. I asked her why that interested her.

'I am interested in everything to do with my father. That's why I came here.'

She inhaled deeply. Quickly pulling herself together, she let the shine come back to her eyes and the smile to her face, and found some theme that was, for her, agreeable. I think she was saying something about how she had seen a Monet exhibition in Stockholm and how he had been, from that time on, her favourite painter. She loved to see how light can change appearances, she said. I did not join in the conversation, and I don't I think she expected me to.

I was thinking about Aleksa; making a quick inventory of my memories. He was a good man. That is, of course, the main thing. His name was Aleksandar Ranković and he did not like it. He did not like being connected to the notorious chief of police who dared to eavesdrop even on Tito, so that immediately after being introduced as Aleksa Ranković, he quickly added: 'Aleksa, as in Šantić, the famous writer'. He wore a moustache which he trimmed every three years, on the very first day of spring. He liked to drink good homemade brandy, and since a person only comes across that very rarely in his life, he was forced to drink ordinary grape brandy; never beer – for it provoked depression in him. When alcohol put him in a good mood he would whisper the Rubaiyat of Omar Khayyam or hum the old pop song, 'You Mean So Much in My Life, Dear'. With a glass in his hand he liked to talk about the erotic episodes in the books of Skender Kulenović and Hamza Humo, and to explain why blondes with long legs and knees slightly turned in on each other have the most erotic walk. And that was it... as much as I could remember... While Mirna was explaining her recently-acquired passion, I was thinking how many things I did not know about Aleksa – the name of his wife, whether he had brothers or sisters, what he was afraid of, whether his parents were alive, what he was like when he became angry and what it was that could most easily make him furious... I had never visited him; I did not even know where he lived. I had never seen him cry, he had never sought help from me, nor did I know which people he liked or did not like in the editorial office... Oh yes, I did know that...

He was a much-appreciated radio reporter. His reports won prizes at the radio festivals and the listeners liked his simple anecdotes about life. Aleksa found interesting characters in factories, in remote villages, suburbs, town settlements: model-makers who fashioned Renaissance buildings from matches, people who made biplanes out of rubbish, collectors of rare butterflies, married couples with ten children who lived in ten square metres of living space, gatherers of myths, former beauties, parapsychologists, transformed criminals, professional miracle-workers, incomprehensible gluttons, fanatical verse-mongers, renowned lovers, pickpockets... You must know this sort of report; many journalists try their hand at it. Yet Aleksa's were different from the rest because he truly liked his characters. He did not fawn upon them, or, God forbid, ridicule them, he talked to them as though he was really interested in their lives, as though he was introducing his friends. The listeners called him 'Our dear Aleksa', they wrote poems to him, sent birthday and New Year felicitations, made enquiries about his health. I think they also liked the way he spoke in the *Ekavian* dialect; his Serbian accent probably reminded them of the popular television series *A Better Life* and *The Hot Wind*. He revelled in their attention and he repaid them with the same enthusiasm. When the war came, he stopped filming reports. A wartime schedule was created, refugees came into the town, only reports from the front were broadcast; testimonials about crimes, notifications of restrictions on electricity and water reductions. There were not even any weather reports. There was no place any more for stories about ordinary people. There were no longer any ordinary people.

I remembered that at the very beginning of the war Aleksa talked a lot, but no longer in a measured way. Once upon a time he had used words carefully, weighed them on his tongue, tried to find the most favourable, even when he was engaged in an incidental conversation; something which I used to like very much. But, during the war, he began to speak quickly, as though he was afraid someone would stop him before he could finish his train of thought. He cursed the national political parties, unfailingly emphasized how those in the leftist party were the worst, that Karadžić and Mladić had ruined his life. At that time, everyone wanted to speak about their own opinions and didn't have any patience for anyone else's. But that talkativeness did not last very long, all at once he shut up, and mostly just listened to others and nodded his head.

And then Mirna was talking... with no trace of Aleksa's accent, again about Sweden, about the cold wind and the cold people, the drunk boats which sailed at the weekend, about tunnels for frogs, lakes and forests. While she was talking she didn't look me in the eye, but instead at a spot between my eyebrows, which made me feel awkward. All at once she stopped, in the middle of a sentence, and said she had to go. While she was tying her trainers in the hallway, I saw that the hair on the back of her head was wet with sweat.[3] She pulled the bow of her shoelaces tight, straightened her trouser legs and said,

'My father was looking for ghosts.'

Then she looked up and asked me, 'Do you believe in ghosts?'

Naturally, I was confused, not expecting such a question on a winter's morning. It seemed to me to be the kind of question to be asked around midnight. But she did not wait for an answer; she already had a new question: 'Can I come tomorrow?'

Again she didn't wait for an answer, as she descended the steps.

Only afterwards, I realised I should have told her that I do believe, not only in ghosts, but also in vampires, werewolves, apparitions, fairies, witches, giants, magicians, astrologers, djinns, dwarfs, *meleke* and angels, *azdaje* and dragons, Satan, Lucifer, *Iblis*, Behemoth, Beelzebub, Astaroth, Gabriel, Azrael, Asmodai, Dzibril, the Holy Grail, sirens, satyrs, unicorns, centaurs, minotaurs, the whole of Borges's fantastic zoo, the Bogeyman, the Golem, Puss in Boots, Baba Yaga... I should have added that I believe in life after death, *Džennet* and Paradise, *Džehennem* and Hell, the Seven Aztec Heavens, Valhalla, Ragnarok, the Eternal Hunting Ground, Hades, Bosch's paintings... and that I have no doubt about the usefulness of Dervish rituals, exorcism, spiritualism, alchemy, the Hodža's notes, cabals, atonements, spell casting, reading tea leaves and coffee grains and animals' intestines, palmistry... That I believe in all magic tricks, levitation, sawing a woman in half, the materialisation of a litter of rabbits from a hat, mass hypnotism, suggestion... And especially, with all my heart, my soul and the remainder of my reason, I believe in reincarnation! For if I didn't believe in reincarnation, in a second chance, I think that depression would suffocate me. As I've already mentioned, it hasn't been easy for me since I started to live alone. It has been hard for me ever since I realised that life will never be beautiful again, as it was before. That no psychology, advice, temptation, folk dancing, or black magic exists which would allow me to once again be happy with my wife. But enough of that for now, for I am in no condition to explain this all to you. But I promise, before the end of this story, I shall relate everything in detail. I just have to be better prepared.

* * *

She did indeed come back the next morning. In a plastic bag she carried a bottle of red wine and a note book with a black leather cover.

'I've come to drink and talk with you. Of course, if I succeed in getting you to start talking. It's easier when there is conversation.'

That frightened me. At that time I didn't like to talk about myself. If I opened my heart to someone, I thought, it would be like officially announcing my condition, as though it will never change. Of course, I was ashamed as well (and you will find out why – the time for that will come too).

'Do you remember why I called you?'

I nodded my head. I was lying, but I was ashamed to admit I had forgotten.

'Help me to find out what happened to my father.'

Like everyone else, I thought that Aleksa had gone to Germany, to meet her and her mother.

'Isn't Aleksa in Germany?'

'No, I haven't seen him since the beginning of '92, when my mother and I left. In March '93, we received a short message from him. He wrote that he was well, that we were not to worry about him and that there were still good people in the world. Everything else was questions: how were we, did we have enough money, had I succeeded in enrolling in school, whether Mama was taking her medicine. That was the last we heard from him.'

'I thought Aleksa had been able to get to Germany. Don't you know what happened to him?'

'I don't know, no-one could say anything about it. Not one little bit of information, until I received this.'

From her bag, she pulled out the notebook and put it on the table.

'You know, father had many notebooks like this, but he would not let me open them. But I still did it, secretly, because I was curious. I never found anything particularly interesting in them, just notes to do with work, written quickly, in abbreviations, often in a completely deformed handwriting. He recorded in a hurry, like journalists often do. But this notebook is completely different.'

I put my hand out for the notebook, but she didn't relax her hold on it. Her palms were shaking on the covers, and she was looking at the centre of the table, like playing a children's game intended to invoke ghosts.

'I remember how he helped us to pack our things. You know, he was never a particularly neat man. But that day, he came into my room and began to fold up a shirt. He worked with special care, slowly doing up the buttons, smoothing out the wrinkles from the material, and then lightly folding it, as though following some plan. Several times he began again from the beginning, until he had finally made a truly perfect square. He reached out for another shirt, but I told him it wasn't necessary, that he would mix up my things, that I could do it myself... I kept on working and I thought he had left the room. But he was standing by the bed and watching every move I made. I held out a T-shirt to him and he took it, quickly, thankfully.'

When she stopped speaking I too had a chance to say something.

I could have told her how my wife came one morning for her things. With her was a man. It was uncomfortable for him too, and as he stood in the hallway, he pushed his hands into his pockets then took them out again straight away, making sure not to look at either me or her. For that reason, I looked at both of them. She was more beautiful than ever, and he was manly and strong, with wide shoulders and a strong chin – just as I had always wanted to look. I liked this sort of man, and she used to say she didn't like them. Now it seemed she was not telling me the truth; or maybe, simply, after everything, she was looking for someone completely different from me. I would have done the same thing. I went into the room and waited for her to finish. I heard them whispering in the hallway, then the lock clicking.

Slowly I came out of the room, locked the door after them and hurried to the bedroom to see for myself that her side of the wardrobe was empty. But inside the flat there were still a lot of things which could remind me of her. For instance, there was the pair of panties that I had most liked to see her wearing. I had hidden them, because I expected that she would come for the rest of her things one day. I didn't think of it as stealing; I bought them for her and had to persuade her to wear them, while she tried to resist, claiming that thongs were extremely uncomfortable. And so I imagined that she wouldn't mind if I kept them with me. Yes, I know, I am calculating, pathetic, egoistic, cowardly... a true modern hero. Maybe this, too, will interest you. At that time I suspected I was becoming impotent, because I looked at all women, no matter how beautiful, only in the eyes. Yet the fact that I constantly imagined my wife's body consoled me. I tried to remember every one of our acts of love, so that every movement, sigh, grimace, even the slightest little curve and bend, were imprinted deeply into my memories. But no matter how hard I tried, I couldn't bring back many memories, only a few short sequences; one wrinkled nostril, two ways of pushing her hair from her forehead, three sighs, one exceptionally beautiful groan...

I did not, of course, relate all this to Mirna, I only said, 'Aleksa was a good man,' and immediately thought I should not have used the past tense.

Quickly I added, 'Shall we drink some wine? It must be room temperature by now.'

She shook her head.

'We don't have time. I have to go, and you have to read.'

She took her hands away from the notebook. On the cover, the imprint of her damp palms was still visible. She got up from the chair to put on her jacket and I jumped up from mine, like a recruit when an officer comes into the room.

While she was tying her laces she said to me, 'I'll come again tomorrow. Please, read the notebook. There's not much... Then we shall talk.'

When I returned to the room, the CD had reached the end. I had the sudden desire to lie down on the bed and to sleep for at least two months, but the notebook was lying on the table. It seemed to me as though it was the centre of the whole flat and that you could see it from every angle. I opened it slowly, as though I was expecting a Jack-in-the box to be pressed between the covers. Yet when I opened it, I realised it wasn't a journalist's notebook at all: neat rows of sentences awaited me, spaced with regular right angles and letters, slightly inclined forward and almost written in a scholastic manner. You can see for yourself... when I got the notebook the first page was blank. The second began with the date...

* * *

10 July 1993

Every time I went with the miners down into the pit, I imagined what would happen if the lift broke loose. The miners felt my fear. Once, one of them put his hand on my shoulder. He wanted to console me. There are wonderful people among them. Much more than in any other profession, it seems to me.

Yesterday, the anxiety was stronger than ever. My hands were shaking, and my mouth was completely dry. Inside my cheeks, big furrows had opened which I could not wet with saliva. The lift set off with a metallic sound, like the clicking of the old-fashioned M48 rifle. The miners around me were breathing noisily down their nostrils.

It began as soon as we left the lift. First, it was the sound that frightened us. From the end of the corridor came little hisses. I looked at the miners; Ragib had red spots on his cheeks, Ibrahim caught himself by the throat, Keli's eyes were wide and he bit his bottom lip. We listened – the hisses turned into squawks, and then we heard blows in the dust, as though heavy raindrops were falling. I thought that from the darkness a narrow carpet of grey plush had been spread with numerous vibrating humps. I was wrong: they were rats! Thousands of them. From the walls of the corridor, between the beams, from the ceiling, it seemed to me from every opening; new ones were jumping out, joining the multitude knocking against our legs. Their claws were scratching on our rubber boots; their tails were whipping our legs. It was horrendous, believe me. One miner, maybe Ragib, called on Allah to help him, and Keli, if you will excuse me, swore out loud: 'We are all going to hell!' I am writing it as it happened, in the raw, so that it can be better imagined.

The wooden frames of the windows were crackling as though in a fire. There was scratching, there was swaying. The ground was escaping under our feet, and deep below us, deep, deep, something inside the earth was raging. Everything was shaking in a terrible fury. It seemed to me that a huge hand had grasped the corridor and was shaking it like a matchbox. It was dreadful. An appalling roar cut through the earth and all the lamps went out. Everything was crashing down around us. Something heavy fell on my shoulders and knocked me to the ground. I heard someone screaming. Another voice, completely changed by fear or pain, screamed: 'Mother dearest!' People were calling for help, it was terrifying. What can a man do in an extremity which is so much greater than he is, than to call for help like a child? Then, all at once, the noise coming from under the earth stopped. The world became calm again. I was lying in the dust, in the dark. But, luckily, I was not alone; I could hear people around me. They were praying. They said their prayers quickly, as though afraid they would not have time to finish them. They wanted to put as many words as possible into one breath; then they breathed in deeply and began again. I thought I would join them, but I didn't know one word of their Muslim prayers. For that matter, I don't know any others either, and I only managed to remember 'God, help me'. But I did not want to cry out loud for help, for I was afraid of destroying the harmony of their prayers, of stopping the magic they were trying to create. I have always been an atheist, but in that darkness and horror and despair, I thought: what if God really exists, what if He can really help? At the same I imagined that, if He does exist, and if He created me, then He would know why I was doing this. He would know that I was doing it solely because of fear of death, and not because of respect and gratitude. If He exists, then He would find me repulsive. Maybe precisely because of that, He would want to crush me underfoot. That is exactly what I thought, I was not myself, you must understand.

And then I heard the stamping of horses' hooves coming from the darkness. I heard neighing too, while the stamping became louder and louder, and they came faster, galloping. I had the impression that at least ten huge horses were coming towards me. I didn't know what to do, I couldn't move, rocks were falling all around me, and a heavy beam was pressing down on me. I think I screamed, very loudly. And then, all at once, the same as when the tape of the recording breaks during a radio broadcast, the galloping stopped. Light came through the darkness. It brightened the palms of my hands first, which I was holding in front of me, as though I were holding a child in them. At the end of the corridor I saw a completely symmetrical circle of light, like you see in the theatre. At first I could make out only shadows, and then the scene became clear. Amazing! In the middle of the light stood a tall, thin man in a long green coat, with a large round collar and black buttons as big as a miner's fist. He had thick, black hair, shining like coal. His face was white, like in a pantomime, his nose narrow, and his eyes did not have any whites, I saw that very well, for they were just little black balls. He bowed to me, and I screamed, because his body broke in half at the height of his chest. He tried to calm me with a smile and by gently nodding his head; he could see I was shaking with fear and some sort of chill which had overcome me. He extended his hand, his right hand, towards me without the possibility of reaching me, as he was nearly ten metres away. Yet even so, I felt his palm on my forehead. It was pleasant, warm; and I immediately stopped shaking, as agreeable tingles spread across my body, seemingly following the same paths through which the blood flows. I looked at him, with gratitude I believe, and his smile changed to a pursing of the lips, then he frowned and let out the sound: 'Gluck auf!' I heard it clearly, and I can say he had a pleasant voice. I didn't know what to say, and the green man leant his head on his left shoulder and looked at me curiously. Children gaze like that: sweetly, as though he was waiting for something, and I did not know what. He smiled again, inclined his head again; while the white light around him became red. He became a black silhouette, like the knight on a chessboard, and then he disappeared. Just like that. As though he had never been there on this earth. Again prayers could be heard. I cannot remember if I heard them while the apparition stood there before me or only afterwards. I began to speak, I said 'People,' but no-one heard me, and only the prayers became louder. Again I spoke and again without any success at all. Just when I had given up trying to call out, a light appeared. Such happiness that was! The light was coming from the pile of stones and earth. We heard the voices of our rescuers. I could see comrades around me. Ragib lifted his head, tears were shining in his eyes. They screamed with happiness, kissed one another, cried. Of course they did: such great happiness it was. Rescue! I asked them if they had seen the green man. I repeated the question, and they just hugged me and kissed me. They were celebrating.

We came through it well; I had a bruise on my shoulder, Keli had broken his arm, and the others had only suffered shock. It was not much.

'You saw Perkman,' Ragib Esrefa Zukić, the oldest worker in the mine, said to me in the clinic. When he saw that I was surprised, Ragib explained to me that I had seen a djinn. And, when I asked him what a djinn was, he answered that it was a supernatural being and again he uttered that word: Perkman. Ragib told me that his father, his grandpa, had told him that Perkman does two things: he can lead you to gold or announce some sort of accident. He asked me when I had seen Perkman, and as soon as I answered him, said that that was strange behaviour for a djinn. Because, he said, Perkman had been late; the misfortune had already happened.

Finally he told me to take care, and when I asked him what to take care about, he replied, an accident, because Perkman must have been warning me about an accident. Good man, Ragib. Poor chap, a true miner. People who live by their own hands are always better than the rest.

11 July 1993

All my life I have avoided writing a diary. I'm not capable of it. Besides, I was afraid that in my old age the pages would sadden me. It would have seemed to me that I had wasted my life. Because of that it was better, I thought, to remember the days I had used up in the way I wanted to, for my nostalgia to make them seem better. But now, for the first time in my life, something completely strange had happened to me. Something worth writing down.

I had to record this experience. It was my first meeting with the supernatural. So it was right to put it down on paper, and then to take my time thinking about it. I had once read about how witches looked after the volumes which they called 'spirit books', which had to have black covers and be written by the author's own hand. My notebook certainly fulfils these requirements.

There are not many people left in the town to whom I can relate my unusual encounter. I cannot tell just anyone about Perkman. Maybe they would think I had gone mad; as it is, they already look at me strangely. I can tell Ahmed, because he believes in such things.

My Anđela would believe me; maybe she could even explain some of it to me. She knew how to calm me down. Mirna would, for sure, listen to me and absorb every word. Even though such a long time has passed, it seems to me that they are still here. That at any moment the door will open. I often think like this. I have to, because it's so hard to think about solitude. Am I really alone?

Today a new editor was appointed at the radio station. I don't know the young man, but it seems to me he is honourable. He gave me ten days off, to free myself from the stress of the accident. While he was talking, through the open window the thunder of cannons was coming from the distance.

12 July 1993

Ahmed understood everything. We sat in his office, in the town library which he has been managing for twenty years. For the same number of years, at the same table, we have been playing chess and sipping our drinks. We still often play now, although without any drinks, because of the war, and the destitution. But, because of this, we play with greater passion than ever! We play in order to escape from this world. The safe logic of chess calms us. It seems to me that I have started to understand the game just as it should be understood. I no longer look at the figures separately; I can look at the board as though it were the world, like an infinite series of possibilities. Ever since I understood that, I have regularly beaten Ahmed.

When I told him about the happenings in the mine, he didn't even ask one question. He only told me not to be afraid, that it was true that Perkman predicted misfortune, but that it was possible to avoid the misfortune if you took his warning and advice seriously.

Ahmed also told me that I would meet Perkman again. When that happened, it would be enough just to return his greeting and to put to him any question I wished.

From the wardrobe, where he keeps his private books, he took out a fat pile of mimeographed notes with the title 'Papers from the Symposium on the Mining and Metallurgy of Bosnia and Herzegovina from Prehistoric Times until the Beginning of the XXth Century' and said to me 'I think you will find some answers there.' That is what he advised me, before calmly beginning to set up the chess pieces.

I have known Ahmed for a long time, a whole eternity, but he always succeeds in surprising me.

13 July 1993

I read Ahmed's mimeographed notes. In the chapter 'On the Origins of the Belief in the Spirit of the Pit, Perkman, in Our Country', Vlajko Palavestra writes that in the villages around the Bosnian mines there exists a specific belief in a wild man, a pit-giant, 'bergmajstor', most often known as 'Perkman'.

Dr Palavestra chronicled the testimony of several miners. In Kreševo, an old man had related that Perkman originated from the soul of a good man, 'that's the soul of a miner who was killed, who comes to work, to help us and make the ore softer'.

The miner Jure Glavočević testified to his experience in 1909. I shall copy it down exactly as it is written:

'One night we went outside, we had a rest hour. And there where we had been working, we forgot something, and as I was the youngest I had to go and get it. I went into the pit and I heard something banging. I run away outside, and an old miner says to me: It was the same with me. I go down into the pit, and a man in a green uniform is standing there in the middle of the tracks, and puts out his hand to take my lamp. But I had heard from the old people that if I meet someone, I must not give him anything from my hand. I put the lamp down on the tracks, he takes it, but I cannot go. He climbs up into the framework of the pit; he looks round at everything, puts the lamp down on the tracks and disappears. He just waved his hand at me, when he left. Later the directors said: The pit will be closed! The next day, everything was destroyed, the whole pit. That man is called the Earth Man, but we call him Perkman.'

14 July 1993

Today, in passing, I heard something I could have easily missed: I heard that in the Music School they are torturing people. I find that hard to believe. At the beginning of the war they were saying that in the football stadium a prison camp for Serbian prisoners had been built, but that was soon shown to be a lie. There are a lot of lies; it is hard to separate the truth from them.

Close to the Music School is the library, next to it is the theatre, and across the road from it is the town cafe. I used to sit there often with Anđela, while we were still talking about getting married. One night, I was hoping that the orchestra would play the song 'You mean so much in my life, dear' by The Red Corals. I wanted this so much that I had already formed the whole scene in my head. I almost convinced myself that it had really happened. But I was disillusioned by the kitsch in that imaginary scene. In it I am dancing dressed in an elegant black suit, like a nobleman from a television series, Anđela is wearing a beautiful white dress, and the orchestra is made up of musicians smiling with all their teeth showing. A completely false picture, because I remember very well, at that time, we were all dressed the same way – in grey or brown suits. Not to mention the teeth of the musicians. That's how it was at that time. Privation. Then again, there was beauty too.

Maybe the comparison is exaggerated, but for similar reasons I can't bring myself to believe in the story about tortured people in the Music School either. Scenes of violent abuse in the practice rooms; next to the instruments, under the portraits of the composers; while the tormentors stamp all over the music books – such scenes make the spectacle exaggerated, even false.

In the mimeographed notes, I found mention of the belief of Serbian miners in the 'Silver Emperor' who sits at the bottom of the mine. One legend says that, when the Turks wanted to take all the silver from the mine, the spirit called upon the rivers Danube and Sava to help. The rivers flooded the valley and so saved the treasure. According to the belief, the 'Silver Emperor' has two helpers, Manul and Dagudin.

15 July 1993

A strange man with blood-shot eyes came to see me. He knocked so gently that I hardly heard him. When I opened the door, he was standing right in the doorway, tightly squeezing the collar of the black coat around his thin neck. I was frightened when I saw that yellow face with huge, blood-shot eyes which stopped me from seeing whether he had a nose, mouth or hair. The direct gaze that he directed straight into my eyes made me afraid that gaze might suck them out. Blood flooded my face and my throat contracted. He looked at me and said that I would never be happy here. As soon as he uttered these words, he turned on his heel and went off down the stairs. Not wanting to watch him go, I quickly shut the door. I thought I would find it hard to forget him, but strangely, last night I slept well.

Ahmed was sad when I related this to him.

I ask myself what he wanted to tell me. Here? Where?

16 July 1993

Karl Gustav Jung noted that a spirit is an active, rapid, agile being who revives, stimulates, animates, inflames with passion and inspires. A spirit, Jung wrote, is a dynamic principle which creates an antithesis to inactivity and movement of matter. It is the contrast between life and death.

Martin Ebon in his small book 'Exorcism' states that, from childhood onwards, Jung met spirits every day. He was closest to a spirit named Philemon, whom he described as a being with the form of an old person, the horns of a bull and wings of a kingfisher.

'Philemon, like the other characters in my visions, clearly let me feel that in my psyche there are things which I do not create, things which appear by themselves and which have their own life. Philemon represents a force which is not me. In my visions I talked to him and he told me things of which I was not aware. I understood very well that he was the one who was talking, and not I.'

I have written it here exactly as Jung noted it down.

17 July 1993

Preparations for the opening of the mine took a long time in our town. A report on the amount of coal in this region was made by the Austrian spy Božić, standard-bearer of the marine regiment. In 1841 the mine administrator, D. Wolf, investigated the presence of coal in the ground, but returned to Vienna after arguing with the other members of his group. To this day, the reason for the disagreement has not been explored. After him, in 1846, Baron Ransonet ascertained that the whole of the central Bosnian basin had an abundance of large coal reserves. In 1879, a group of geologists, among them E. Mojsilowich, E. Tietze, A. Bittner and Professor Hoernes, made the first geological map of this area.

Finally, the mine was opened on the fifth of May, 1880, registered to the Viennese firm 'Kohlen Industria Verein'. By 1895, 295 miners and six machines of 200 horsepower were working in the coal mine, extracting 620 thousand tonnes of coal.

Right next to the mine a settlement, or colony, was established, which in 1905 contained 40 workers' houses, seven homes for supervisors, two pretty houses for office workers, a small hospital and a group bathing-place. For a long time the Germans remained in control of the business, and the names of the first directors have been recorded: Richter, Karbon and Poech.

Now a new column of refugees has come into town. Trucks, buses, horses and carts and muddy automobiles passed slowly through the streets. The people in the vehicles did not speak to one another, I noticed instantly; for they were looking intently at the town. I think they want to take in every street, window, passer-by, and to compare them with all that they have left behind. In return, the passers-by hid their glances.

I noticed that the pigeons have completely lost their faith in people. It is impossible to get nearer than five metres to any one of them.

18 July 1993
I shall never forget the phantom gallop I heard in the mine. I found the notes of Baron Rudolf Maldini Wildenhainski, who visited our mine in 1900. It was the fate of the horses which worked beneath the ground that impressed him the most. He noted:

'Well, in all the collieries there is not one steam engine. In many of them the coal is brought to the lift by horses, and in others by people, so that in bigger collieries you will find that this job is done by one hundred and more horses, which are kept in stables 200–300 metres deep in the ground. Since these horses mostly are kept at a stable, warm temperature all the time, they are usually of a good countenance. They are brought to the surface only when they are no longer able to do the job, or else when they are no longer necessary. These horses always follow the same path, so that they know the way very well. It happens that freely moving horses two kilometres away from their underground path go alone in the dark to find their place in the stable. It is an arduous and dangerous job, that of miners in the depths of the earth, where their lives are constantly at risk. For this reason they always greet one another with "God give us good luck!"'

In the pit I heard the souls of the unfortunate; those blind horses! It was the gallop that these poor beasts were dreaming about in the heavy darkness that had frightened me.

19 July 1993

Ahmed told me that in folklore there is a belief that a mine acquires a soul, and therefore a protector, when the first miner is killed in it. His bones are put into a blind trench which is then filled in and forgotten. It is for this reason that, after the ceremonial opening of the pit, while women adorn the opening with special decorations and regale the engineers with pies and cakes, the first miners go down into the pit while reciting the most powerful prayers. They look at one another suspiciously and try to judge who will be killed. Because, they know, someone must, in order for it to be well for the others. If that does not happen, the vein very soon gives out, and the mine shuts down.

It is obvious that my mine had its human sacrifices, because it has been working for so many years. It is only the open-cut mine that was closed very soon after the opening. This is where the local peasants throw the surplus puppies and kittens born to their dogs and cats.

20 July 1993

Every day some new thing reminds me of Anđela. Today I moved the bed and behind it I found a small striped sock. Every garment that the two of them used has a very strong effect on me. Like electricity going through my body and throwing pictures in front of my eyes. This time I saw how Anđela used to sit on the bed in the mornings and quickly pull on those socks, because the parquet floor was cold. In them she pattered to the bathroom, and then to the kitchen, while I pretended to be asleep and listened to the clattering of the dishes.

When this short film finished, I was seized by a feeling of faintness.

The sock finished up in the box, together with the other things which bring back memories. I pushed the box into the pantry, at the bottom of the shelves, along with the other things waiting until someone needs them.

21 July 1993

In Germany there is a traditional tale about the underground spirit of the mines, who appears in the form of a dwarf known as Bergmann. People must greet Bergmann with 'Gluck auf'; and they are cheerful, dancing before their king, who helps poor miners to dig up as much coal as possible. In Thuringia, they abide by the tradition that the miners must first greet the spirit when they encounter him, after which he will be kindly towards them. In Silesia, they believe that his greeting must on no account be returned, for if it is it will precipitate some accident on the miner who received the greeting, and on the whole group.

Last night, Anđela sat next to my bed. I am not sure if I dreamt it. She was sad, and I am afraid something terrible had happened. Exactly six months ago I received the last message from them. On the Red Cross document it said only that they were well and that they had at last moved into a rented apartment. They added their new address and told me to contact them as soon as possible. I tried, I sent messages with people who were leaving the town, but I heard nothing back from them. I am afraid. I am not sure what I am afraid of, but I am truly afraid.

If I meet Perkman or Bergmann again, whatever his name, I shall ask him to tell me how the two of them are. I shall try tomorrow to go down into the pit.

22 July 1993

At the editorial meeting I said that I was preparing a big story about the mine. The new editor is enraptured with the idea, saying that it is important for the morale of the townspeople and the soldiers to create at least the illusion that industry is working normally. Because of this, he has freed me from all other obligations on the radio.

However, I did not succeed in going down into the mine, for the director would not allow me to go. He is a good man, his name is Vernes, but everyone calls him 'the Ant'. He told me that, if I was anywhere in the vicinity, the miners would refuse to even approach the mine. Terrible! And yet I understood what it was all about, and why the miners were behaving like that. I had almost become accustomed to it. Whenever they announce some evil deed perpetrated by the Serbian army on the radio, or when a shell kills someone, my neighbours stop greeting me in the corridor, and in the office there is a sudden silence when I come into the room. Until now, I had not noticed this with the miners. They even used to call me their comrade. I asked Ant why they had changed. He said that in the mine they had heard that I had seen the spirit who announces misfortune and so the miners were afraid that something bad would happen to them if I went in with them.

Ant apologized, he said they would get over it, and I turned around without saying anything, and went out. But I knew that I must see Perkman again, in order to be convinced that I did not dream him. I must talk to him.

In the library, I found 'Introduction to Demonology'. I think I have succeeded in finding in it the origin of my Perkman. He is an 'elemental', a gnome or demon being: the ugly dwarf who minds the treasure of the underworld.

It says in the book that Paracelsus believed that the earth was ruled by 'Elementals': mythical beings who rule the elements. Elves controlled fire, ondines ruled the water, and gnomes were masters of the earth. Paracelsus warned that one must not confuse Elementals with demons and stated that wizards gained valuable information from them, especially to do with the characteristics of the elements.[4]

Last night I left a full glass of water on the little table by the bed. This morning it was empty.

23 July 1993

When I die I want to be cremated. Then they can climb the tallest building in town and wait for some wind and shake out my ashes. I do not want to lie in the ground. I do not want any piece of ground to have my name on it. I have had enough of this place. I can't stand it any longer. It all makes me want to vomit. I want to be gone, to be forgotten. That is the best way. What's the sense of us all living in misery?

Anđela was again sitting next to my bed, just above the pillow. I heard her breathing and I smelt her perfume. But I pretended I was asleep, so she wouldn't disappear again. Unfortunately, in the end I did drop off.

The morning was white and my eyes hurt from the strong light.

24 July 1993

Once again, the man with the blood-shot eyes visited me. Just as before, he stood in the doorway and said: 'You will never be happy here'. After saying this sentence he opened his eyes even wider, turned around, lifted his hand and with a thin finger pointed at a small figure leaning on the handrail of the steps. I saw a small girl, probably about 12 years old. I only saw her for a short time, from the back. She had blond hair with a ponytail. She went quickly down the steps. I asked the man to tell me who she was.

He lifted his gaze to the level of my forehead, and I saw his little mouth. His mouth opened, he took a breath of air as if he wanted to tell me. And then, it was as though someone grabbed him by the hand and took him away from the door. He turned quickly and ran down the steps.

Muslims think djinns are beings of steam or fire, who can appear in different forms. They are made out of flames without smoke, while people and angels are made from clay and light. They believe that djinns too can be saved, that the Muslim prophet Mohammed was sent for them as well as for ordinary people.

And so some of them will be sent to Paradise, and others will burn in Hell. In the Islam of law schools, they claim that a man who dies in mortal sin can be turned into a djinn.

25 July 1993

Children are not afraid of death. Today I saw a group of children squeezing onto the wall above the river, while below them, in the shallows, the body of a man was swaying back and forth. His legs had been cut off close to his knees, and blue veins were sticking out from the stumps. Water weed and cigarette butts were entangled in the hairs on his chest and around his genitals. The children were shouting: 'A dead man! A dead man, a dead man!' They even called the passers-by over with their little hands so as to look them in the eyes. They seemed satisfied if they could see horror, or at least disbelief, there. The police, gathered on the shore, held their handkerchiefs to their mouths. The children were copying them even though the smell could not possibly have reached them as far as the top of the wall. Adults would turn their heads away when they saw the corpse, and then squint over their shoulders; but the children kept their eyes wide open. Yet they did not get down from the wall even when the medical orderlies took away the body. When their mothers started to call them from their windows the children answered: 'Let us stay longer, just a little, a little more, it's not dark yet, we only just started to play.'

26 July 1993

An unusual day. I met a beautiful, young girl. Ahmed brought her into the library while I was leafing through the archives of the local newspapers. He said the girl had an interesting story for me. She was embarrassed, and stains of red covered her cheeks. But they were not in the slightest bit ugly; they were pretty and full of life...

She told us that her grandfather lived in the little town of F., where she often went for her school holidays. He was an old miner and he used to put her to sleep with stories of the time when the mine was full of gold. He told her that, while the vein of gold was rich, hundreds of Perkmen pushed themselves into the mine, and talked to the miners and helped them. When they knocked three times on the floor that meant that soon new gold would be found. Four knocks meant misfortune was coming close and that all the miners must quickly leave the pit. But as the gold became increasingly less and less, fewer and fewer

Perkmen could be seen in the mine. Only one stayed, and he was a drunkard, so that the miners spilt home-made brandy on the floor for his pleasure.

While the girl was talking, I wanted to hug her, to thank her. She was young and life was still scintillating around her. If such a luminous being can be interested in the spirits in mines, then my search is not strange, or senile, or senseless. Then I am not alone. But as soon as she had finished her story, she told us she had to go because the next day she was leaving town. As she left the library, Ahmed and I watched her go; leaning on the boards of the wooden tables, cold in the middle of summer.

27 July 1993

Bergier wrote about the demons who announced themselves to Renaissance scientists, cabalists and Islamic mystics. He calls them 'beings of light' and states that they appeared most often in the first centuries following the start of Christianity, and then again, after a long pause, they came back among men at the end of the 13th and the beginning of the 14th century. He believes the beings of light caused the fire during the time of the great plague in London, so that the epidemic would not extend to the rest of the world.

When I notice female beauty I feel disgust towards myself. Every such glance I experience as a betrayal of my only beautiful ones, Anđela and Mirna. I heard that people discover new passion in themselves during war, that fear of death is a strong aphrodisiac. I look only at women's eyes. Nothing else interests me.

28 July 1993

Allah created this world so that it would be pleasing to an intelligent seven-year-old boy. That is what Ahmed said to me when I left his office.

I think the thing that He made best was the morning. How I used to love the morning! I loved to drink coffee with Anđela and to make arrangements for the day, while morning was coming into the room. I loved every one of our conversations. I loved the little movements of her fingers around the cup. The scents, the clock ticking, the news on the radio... my whole body would relax. I could be alone with her for days, with her and the child in that little room. I used to tell her even prison would not be hard for me if we were together. Because, as the proverb says, if the household is never spiteful, the house is never too small.

Mornings are now completely senseless. I imagine that they are still beautiful, but I can no longer notice.

30 July 1993

In a notebook I found my old list of terrors. I made it several years ago, just for the sake of it, after I read in the daily newspaper the advice of some psychologist who stated that in the fight against different phobias the most important thing was to admit they existed. My list had seven terrors:

- Fear of death;
- Fear of illness;
- Fear of poverty;
- Fear of reptiles;
- Fear of large bodies of water;
- Fear of heights;
- Fear of being buried alive.

While I was reading this list I realised I had resolved all the fears, except one, the last on the list – fear of being buried alive. Anthropologists claim that this fear was only born in the eighteenth century and that it was the first form of the fear of death to be accepted. In the middle of the eighteenth century doctors drove needles under the nails of the dead, poked pencils into their nostrils, pushed horse manure or urine or medications which caused sneezing under their noses. They did all this to avoid the responsibility for that dreadful awakening in the dark of the grave. Chopin, Schopenhauer, Renoir, Andersen, Dostoyevsky and Nobel all requested that before burial their arteries be cut, so that they could be certain they would not be buried alive.[5]

Today I added to the list one more fear – the fear of solitude.

I am afraid. That psychologist was not right. Fears are like vampires, they appear when you talk of them too often.

For the rest of the day I was thinking about Anđela and Mirna. I am still thinking about them now.

31 July 1993

I have found some people who can help me in all the important ways: to allow me to meet Perkman again and to see Anđela and Mirna. They are two brothers, arrogant, but with excellent connections in the town. We are not friends, but they will help me for a good price. I hope I will be able to get together enough money, for I am ready to sell everything I have.

Ahmed says the brothers remind him of Jedžudž and Medžudž, those two mythical figures whose appearance will announce the coming of Judgement Day. Some Muslim teachings believe they originated from the first man, Adam, coming from his semen when it flowed from him during the night and then mixed with the earth. Tradition says that they are strong people who are impossible to kill. Ahmed says that the appearance of Jedžudž and Medžudž has been recorded: wide faces like forged shields, small eyes, red hair. They really do look like them.

But the thing that frightens Ahmed the most is that the red-haired brothers are criminals who suddenly became rich after the beginning of the war.

I consoled him, I told him that maybe they were my Manul and Dagudin.

1 August 1993

I don't have many things which could be valuable at this time. My books and a few paintings that were not signed by anyone popular, and so are quite worthless. I made Anđela take her jewellery with her and now I am happy because of that, for I do not have to think about selling it. I think I can get some money for the household appliances, and the Volkswagen I hid from mobilization in Ahmed's garage will come in handy too,

I told my guides to take me to the one place where you can meet Perkman. Of course, I did not explain to them why I was going there, and neither did they ask.

I am going tonight. They told me I must not speak to anyone about it. Still, I told Ahmed. I could not leave him without saying goodbye. We kissed one another (as is the custom). I placed the key to my flat in his fist. He stood on the steps of the library and watched me go. I turned around bowed and said: 'Gluck auf'. He did not smile.

* * *

In order to read the text from the notebook, slowly, and with only a few pauses, you would need at the most an hour. It took me all night. Aleksa's book of ghosts was like a mirror: I seemed to recognise myself in it and that agitated me greatly. I felt the same fears as Aleksa, the same longing, the same emptiness, loneliness, depression... I'm sure that you can understand what it was like for me to read about the man with the big eyes, the objects on slides, spirits both earthly and non-earthly... My vest, I remember, was completely wet with sweat, sticky and thick, like the caramel for *baklava*. I was afraid, nervous, shocked, sad, curious, furious... Heavy subject matter like that seems to press down on me, my stomach quivers, a headache starts from the middle of my skull, scrapes and sand-papers bones and meat. I didn't have any caffeine tablets left in the flat to cure my headache; during nine months I had used up my supply. Only those tablets could calm my headaches down, one glance at their golden packaging was enough to make me feel like a grounded person.

I placed my head in my hands, carefully, as though it were not mine. I sat down and waited for Mirna. I felt as though I were naked in an icy wind. Like a father in the waiting room of the maternity ward. Like the person executing the decisive penalty. Like a man expecting a ghost.

Outside the snow had stopped falling.

I listened. Silence. Complete. I could not hear even the smallest sound. Even the refrigerator was not humming. The walls were quiet: all six sides of my box. As though the flat was out in space, or under the earth, and not in a multi-storey building with cardboard walls, busy water pipes, squeaking mechanized lift... As though I were not stuck in a building with eighteen floors each with four apartments full of people on each of them. If the apartments were arranged into small houses and placed in a field, next to a stream, near a forest, under some hills, there would be a village of quite considerable proportions which would deserve a dot on the geographic map. The residents of my multi-storey building could have in that village their own customs, celebrate strange saints or keep the secrets of some traditional skill – fascinating embroidery, horse-training or wine-making. They could even have a special language; maybe even squeal while they laugh. The women could sing lascivious songs together while they beat their washing in the stream, and the men spend their evenings in ancient and moronic little games... In a village like that silence would be impossible, even in the middle of the night; dogs would be barking, their chains would be rattling, the animals in the stables would be mooing, neighing or whatever they like to do, chickens would be quaking in front of predators and under roosters, lovers would jump fences, there would be fortune-tellers casting spells, children whispering under the covers... A complete and utter silence like this would mean that the village was deserted, that there was nothing alive in it, that some misfortune had swooped down on it and smothered it.

As I sat there, it suddenly crossed my mind to doubt whether they had all gone to work? It was impossible to imagine that every neighbour had some sort of job to do outside, that in the apartments there was not one housewife, pensioner, or child... Or some idler like me, who lived off the collection of rent for inherited business premises? Where are all those hordes of bill collectors, tax men, burglars and beggars? Is it possible that nobody is entering into our apartment building, that no-one is using the lift? That all the inhabitants of the seventy-two boxes had been struck dumb at the same time and decided not to move from their own territory? Impossible, of course, everyone cannot possibly be sitting in their rooms and sifting through their lives... Someone has to be filling up the days about which others will be thinking. Someone has to fight, so that others have enough room for complaining and doing nothing.

I was waiting for Mirna, and yet I did not know when she would come. I also did not know how I would spend the time until she came. Normal people would have breakfast, eight o'clock in the morning being the time for a methodical civilian meal. But I could not eat; because of Aleksa's notebook my stomach was cramped, I could hardly even swallow air. I had to think of something, something to do, anything. Otherwise, I knew with certainty, I would pick up the telephone. The last time I had done that I had been confined to bed for exactly nine months and three days. Even thieves in our country get a lighter sentence than that, and I had even prescribed solitary confinement for myself. I begin to sweat when I remembered that conversation.

I remember, very well, how I begged her to return to me. In the beginning I put on a firm voice, acted as though I were a reasonable and mentally concentrated person, I even brought forth arguments... As soon as I felt her cold, and until then unknown to me, inflexibility, I started to become hysterical, to list everything I had ever done for her, all the times she had hurt me... I switched to abusing her, accused her of being unfaithful during our whole marriage, of leaving me because we were having a financial crisis, counted all the women with whom I could have slept but did not because of her. She put down the receiver and turned off the telephone... It was only then that I remembered that, while I was preparing the conversation, I had planned to use the sentence that John Malkovich said to Debra Winger in *The Sheltering Sky* – 'To love for me means to love you'. I thought that sentence could help me, could soften her...Now I am sure it would not have done so, it would only

43

have made my entreaties more pitiful. Not long ago in *Lolita* I found the part where Humbert Humbert pleads with the girl to come back to him. I shall write it for you:

'Are you completely sure that – all right, it's understood, not tomorrow, and not the day after tomorrow, but – well, one day, whenever, you won't come to live with me? I shall create a completely new god and thank him with piercing cries, if you give me just that microscopic hope' (or something like that).

'No, she said, smiling, no.'

I had read *Lolita* carefully, twice I think, but I had not noticed this part. When I accidentally came across it, it shocked me completely. Nabokov was surgically precise – an unreasonable entreaty and a rational reply. One of our conversations evolved just like that; I did not mention creating a god, but I pleaded for a grain of hope. And that is the same.

I could not allow myself another telephone conversation like that. I could not go through the same tunnel again. Aleksa's story was a much better way to go. I did not know what Mirna wanted from me, but I yearned to become a part of that story, to immerse myself completely in it, to learn the ending. It was not just idle curiosity, at least not only that... I was looking for some meaning in life, something to occupy me... and I felt that the black notebook had come into my life at the right time.

In order to shed light on the secret completely, I decided to search through every day of Aleksa's diary.

Mustafa was shouting under the window. I could not hear clearly what he was saying, because the motor of some car in the car park was coughing like a dying person. I made out only: 'We are the inspiration'... Knowing he would repeat it, I jumped up out of the chair, I quickly opened the window, in one moment the cold air dried the sweat from my forehead, and I heard: 'Mustafa has spoken', and then the motor let out a roar again. Mustafa went away to the next building, and I desperately watched him go.

The first time I saw him was just after the war. He worked at the town marketplace, emptying the crates from trucks at dawn. After his work, at exactly 8.30, he made a circuit of the area around the marketplace. He walked in front of the apartment buildings, quickly as though on important business, then stopped suddenly, raised his head towards the windows and shouted: 'Mustafa has spoken'. After that announcement a message would follow, a different one every day. For three months, as I was lying in bed, I did not miss one. Some I can still remember: 'There was not enough accommodation during the war'; 'Everyone is to blame, no-one is innocent'; 'Many things happen and it is hard to pay so much attention just to one'... Once he said: 'The world is making a new arrangement and everything remains the same'. If I had had the energy and the desire, I could have written down the messages, to analyse them and find in them principles, meaning, motive... Unfortunately, I did not. I was told that once Mustafa went up to the market, customers slowly aimed his index finger at the head of each one of them and said: 'You, you, you and you, you will end up in Hell.' They burst out laughing, and one of them said: 'What, me too Mustafa? I bought you a meat pie a little while ago; you could have left me out of it.' Mustafa looked at him seriously and calmly replied: 'I can't help you. I don't ask questions about that.'

Until then I had taken no notice of his messages, but that morning it seemed to me that he spoke only to me.

I can't remember how much time passed until Mirna arrived. I know I was sitting in front of the notebook and studying Aleksa's handwriting. I had once read Ludwig Klages's book on graphology so I thought I could come to some conclusions. Of course, I concluded nothing, except for the fact that I liked the way Aleksa wrote his flowing letters – correctly and decisively, with thick ink at the beginning of the straight part and just a touch of blue at the end. Simple, and yet decorative. Stylish. I tried to remember the image of Aleksa, to recall him from memory. I was surprised how well I succeeded, seeing him almost as though he were standing in front of me. Like a holograph projection in a SF series. He was tall, half a head taller than I, a little stooped, yet he always looked people in the eye. I don't remember ever seeing him run. Someone told me that in his youth Aleksa had been an amateur actor and that he was the first Hamlet in our town. I believe that, for he had a dignified bearing, almost humorously stiff, like people who have never met a nobleman expect a nobleman to be. His hair was cut short, and was coarse and completely white, as was the thick moustache which covered his lower lip. He smoked strong cigarettes, without a filter, but his moustache was always a sterile white, without any touch of nicotine yellow. What else? When he sat down, he gently lifted the legs of his trousers with his fingers. So that the material would not stretch at the knees, I presume. While he talked he would finger the big Adam's apple at his throat, and when he was thinking he would pinch the skin of it.

I tried to remember all those details about Aleksa's person, and I succeeded unexpectedly well. And yet I cannot now remember how Mirna arrived. All I know is that she was suddenly standing in the hall, quite serious, and that she was looking directly into my eyes. Just like her father did. She nodded her head, presumably satisfied with what my troubled gaze could tell her, and asked:

'Will you help me to find my father?'

All at once, I felt a strength. At last. It was a good feeling, to be strong, self-confident and manly, like the leader of the National Party. I said, with an admirable, steady voice:

'Of course.'

With a wide movement of my arm I indicated she should come into the apartment. Into the lair of the awakened badger. I squeezed her shoulders with my hands, looked into her eyes and made sure to keep my voice steady while I promised I would do everything necessary to help her. Mirna fitted perfectly into this scene from a television series. She was elated; she hugged me around the neck and leant her breasts against me. I found it pleasant. Soft.

Warm. Alive. Looking up at me from below, under my chin, she asked me when I would start.

'Tomorrow, straight away tomorrow, there's no time to lose. Actually, tonight, I'll start tonight,' I announced decisively. And basked in her admiring gaze.

I was hoping we would, after everything, in the tranquillity following the utterance of the promises, sit and open that bottle of wine. And that then, radiant with awakened masculinity, I would outline the strategies of the search. But, Mirna kissed me on the cheek, said she would contact me very soon, and left me standing in the middle of the room. Confused. And perhaps this was a better way; because I actually didn't have any plan at all.

First of all, I had to find a way to get through the night. It seemed to me that the best thing would be to continue to try to regain my strength and train for my return to society. I showered, found clean clothes, waited until there were not too many people in the street, and went then out. The sky was dark, like fresh asphalt. Wrapped in a scarf and with a cap pushed down to my eyebrows, I wanted to look like the Invisible Man.[6] That was the best way; I had got to know that role very well.

* * *

During our five years of marriage, I had firmly believed that my wife was stifling my freedom, and considered that my life, without marriage vows, would have been much better and more exciting. Often at night I stood by the window, while she was sleeping, and observed how the town was living. Without me. I counted all the lighted windows, imagined those exciting sleepless people, who surely had not put on pyjamas and then watched the evening film. I listened to the clamour from the kafana, enjoyed bits and pieces of songs and laughter. By day, even while she was holding my hand, I sneaked looks at pretty women in the street and imagined they were sending me secret signals. In my head I made lists of beauties with whom I would never sleep. I kept in mind those who were not accompanied by men, and especially those who looked at me. I thought about the fact that the whole country was full of exceptionally beautiful beings, in every canton, on both sides of the inter-entity line. I was sure that sad, lonely women were just waiting to hear my story and to delight in the jokes which had made my wife laugh with such gusto at the beginning of our relationship. And what about the female situation in the neighbouring countries? They seemed to offer complete luxury; debauchery in the pool of culture we once used to share. In the rich and continually peaceful states were many women who would surely translate every silence of mine as the consequence of war trauma and unselfishly try to console me. In my imagination, beauties from exotic countries were also dancing, some of them wild and aggressive, some because of their traditionally submissive roles, others genetically gifted with figures conforming to men's most ardent desires. That's how I used to daydream.

When my wife left me,[7] everything changed. Beautiful women still walked by me, but they no longer noticed me. I tried to catch their eye, yet when I succeeded I wasn't happy with their reaction. They understood my staring as an attack, an insult. Some of them arrogantly returned my gaze and disdainfully wrinkled their pretty little noses. Most of them just looked straight through me. As though I were not there. Or more accurately, as though I were transparent. An invisible man, as I said before.

I needed to meet a woman. I decided to start going out regularly, to the very same bar I used to visit before I was married: The Sevens.

It looked the same. The walls were still decorated with posters of The Magnificent Seven, Snow White and the Seven Dwarfs, The Seven Samurai, The Seventh Seal; the same chairs; the same ashtrays. The clients were the same too. Most of them were those of my generation who were still left alive. They came every night, though I couldn't imagine that one man would have been ready with the appropriate arguments to explain why he liked that place. The owner was overbearing; behaving as though he was running a multinational corporation, not a small café-bar. I remember once when one of my friends (former friends of course), asked him how he managed to choose precisely the worst songs from the record collection, and he very seriously replied:

'I don't put music on for fools like you. I choose songs that girls might like. And you, whatever I put on, you will come because of them.'[8]

And he was right.

It was because of women that I too returned to that wretched place. Remorseful. Because for years I had tried to lock people out of my life. Deliberately. I couldn't bear social obligations, any sort of responsibility. I could hardly bear the physiological needs with which I was forced to comply. It was not hard to detach myself from the world; I only had to get rid of a handful of friends and a few relations. A touch of arrogance, a few broken promises and failed expectations was enough to do the trick. The telephone was struck dumb. I was happy.

But that evening, when I peered like a weasel into The Sevens, I desperately needed company. It proved successful, even that first evening, with me sneaking myself into some quite attractive female company. I began a conversation with a few remarks about the other customers and they answered admirably, laughing while throwing out their chins; seemingly alone for too long, they seemed to appreciate old-fashioned courtship. After that, I decided to show that I was not only witty, but also clever, so I talked about literature, purposefully mentioning writers whose books I presumed they had not read, with such comments as: 'Céline best described the comedy of despair' or 'Džamonja was the only one who knew the essence of the short story'.

As soon as I noticed their attention was wandering I hurried with drinks so as to reduce my nervousness and loosen my tongue. Indeed, my brain relaxed, but my tongue tied itself up in knots. My observations became most unusual, but at the same time incomprehensible. After a couple of drinks and fifteen minutes, everything became vague. The girls started looking around the kafana, while I took their hands and tried uselessly to gain back their attention. Another booze-filled half an hour passed, until I finally began to cry. Yes, I did, profusely... My tears fell onto the table while I talked about my wife and explained how I had been brutally left alone, deserted, totally helpless without her, miserable, useless, invisible. I murmured through my tears and when I wiped them away I saw that the girls had left the table. In a friendly manner, the waiter whispered in my ear that it would be good if I rested for a while at home. I obeyed him.

The next day I decided I would drink much more carefully and sit by myself. However, that didn't turn out to be a good idea, either. I had the feeling that everyone was looking at me, retelling the scene from the night before and whispering to each other how terrible it was that in so many years I had not succeeded in making even one friend.

The following night I found a place in the corner... No, that was not how it was, I tried once more. I found some old acquaintances and went out with them. I thought that with them I would gain self-confidence and restore the rhythm of going out. It turned out to be a mistake, it was an uncomfortable experience. It seems they were bitterer than I and had understanding only for the relationships at the betting shop. They despised all the customers, especially the ones they greeted most warmly, made fun of every weakness, belittled every attempt to succeed. I realised I didn't have the strength for them.

So, after that I found a place by myself in the corner. I sat in the esteemed position, from where the regular customers could see the whole scene, while at the same time keeping an eye on the street and monitoring the entrance of new customers. There I was, installed like a security camera, drinking slowly and watering down the alcohol, to ward off drunkenness and tone down the hangover. In that crowded room, I was completely alone. I don't think I even need to explain; the relationships in such places are understood: people come in because of their need to be with other people, and then they pretend not to notice one another. The night passed without any major unpleasantness. In fact, it was almost pleasant.

Yet it only took until the next evening for me to have had enough of everything. I hated the customers in the kafana, the staff, the posters on the walls, the ashtrays, the newspaper stand, the air refresher, the narrow cupboards, the choice of music, the shape of the glasses, the empty Complaints Book, the calendar, the lamps, the free postcards and the football club scarf displayed behind the bar, the tiles, the panelling, every crevice, the mirror. I apologize if I've forgotten something that I hated more than these things already mentioned. Like a gas bottle with a weak valve, I sat in the corner, drank, and watched people. They had completely filled up the little café-bar, the walls were bursting. Some strange anger, like I had never felt before, completely consumed me. My jaws were stiff with its force. I tried to discern where the anger came from, and I think I can even put it into percentages:

50% alcohol
+
10% exposure to stress
+
10% physical and psychological weakness
+
10% fear of solitude
+
5% fear of the future
+
5% bad day for weather forecasters
=
Outbreak of senseless yet unstoppable anger.

I shouted: 'Fuck you all!'
No-one noticed me, so I broke my glass on the floor and yelled again, so loudly this time that my eye sockets hurt;
'Fuck you all!'

At last they all looked at me. The waiter came up with a sympathetic smile, and I swung my unsteady arm at him. The slap threw his head right back. Someone turned the music off; strong arms took hold of me and conveyed me outside. I struggled, with no success. The bouncers were laughing and jokingly trying to calm me down as though I were an agitated boy. The short owner of the café-bar stood before me. His five minutes had arrived. I was his Oscar, his Grammy award, his Olympic gold; I was a substitute for the glances of love-sick girls, the cries of admiring men, ovations reverberating in the sport stadium, the chanting at rock concerts... I was the Grail for him; Nazi gold; a gold Diners Club card. Sensually, he closed his eyes while he gave me two smacks across my face: elegant, noisy and juicy. I saw the rapture in his eyes - clear, one hundred per cent, unclouded by anything: multivitamin-induced, absolutely natural, super adrenalin satisfaction. He was shining like a magnificent comet separating two epochs. It was an unforgettable experience to be a part of that. After the punches he wiped his little hands on his trousers, smoothed his hair and deeply sighed. For a moment I was afraid he would say: 'These slaps hurt me more than you', but he did not, he said something even worse:

'This is for your own good. Go home and sober up, and we'll forget everything that happened. You can come back here, but don't let this happen again. '

He knew how lonely I was! He knew that his café-bar was the only place where I could meet people! He had smelt my own fear of loneliness! The realisation of that hurt me much more than any blow. It hurt me that my fear was so conspicuous, that it could be read like an open book. I wanted to tell him he was wrong, that he didn't know me at all, that I could easily be alone, totally and forever.

Those three had gone back into the bar, and I had stayed where I was as further entertainment for the kafana public. An icy wind had taken over from the slapping, entered into my head and added to the displacement of my already perverse thoughts. I heard a car horn. Ekrem leant out of the window of his taxi and called loudly for me to get in. I don't know how much of the performance he had seen, but he only remarked, 'It seems, neighbour, that Ekrem's famous sour soup would do you good.'

As soon as I got into the car, the familiar surroundings helped me to feel a little calmer. I had often used Ekrem's services, because I had never passed my driver's test. I don't remember ever seeing him worried; he seemed to be able to find an adequate solution to any problem. There was a time when the newspapers were full of stories of attacks on taxi drivers. All the drivers in town were anxious and had begun to arm themselves. At the taxi rank they would compare whose measures of protection were the most efficient, and then asked Ekrem what weapon he had obtained. Calmly, he answered that in the boot of the car he had the handle of a shovel. When one of them observed that the attackers would be able to kill him three times over before he had time to get to the boot, he replied

'Maybe they can; but when Ekrem finally gets to the boot at last...'

While we were eating the soup, he asked me, 'Not easy without the missus, is it?'

I made no answer; presuming he could see by the state of me that it was not much fun. He seemed to expect just such a response, because he immediately began expounding the advantages of a bachelor life. I shall try to reconstruct his theory.

'I have been married three times and besides my wives I've had numerous lovers. I just decided one day not to tie myself down any more. There's going to be no more love for me. I give to no-one, and ask nothing from anyone. And since that time, I am a new man, born again. I visit my former wives, I go to see the children, I have a lover, but I don't allow any one of them to have coffee in my apartment, much less to sleep overnight. Understand?'

His apartment seemed a cold place, bare like a furniture salon. He had two armchairs, a chair, a closet and carpet. And nothing else, not one object, newspaper, piece of paper. Nothing. I was freezing, my head was ringing with the smacks, and my forehead was burning, my ears ringing. But Ekrem did not expect an answer.

'I wouldn't change my single life for anything. I make all my own decisions, right or wrong. I do only what I want and only have to look after myself. If I have to satisfy my bodily needs, you know what I mean; there are heaps of women around. If a man is lazy, there are always whores, and every video shop has plenty of porn.'

He imagined my questions and gave answers to them. While he spoke, he gesticulated wildly with his hands; probably not knowing what to do with them in the absence of the steering wheel.

'I make sure I don't fall in love. While my first wife was in the maternity ward, I brought my mistress home. I had to, understand? Not because of the sex, but because I had begun to realise how much I was afraid for her. A clever man doesn't need that.'

I remained silent, so he put his hand on my shoulder, waited patiently for me to lift up my head from the plate and then uttered the concluding remark:

'The main rule is that you do not attempt to fill the emptiness that is left after one woman leaves. You have to turn away from your old life and make a completely new one. Just for you, like you want it! Understand?'

At that moment I understood nothing. I only felt confused, as though everything in me had changed places. I clenched my jaw tightly, so that it wouldn't start to shake from the cold that had come over me. It was as though I had stepped out into a storm, which had seeped into my head and mixed up every sensible thought. All sorts of things occurred to me; I even thought about suicide. Why not, I had enough reasons? The cook at the French court in the seventeenth century, François Vatel, had killed himself simply because he had not been able to secure fish from the North Sea for a feast. And I was lonely, desperate, humiliated: which are obviously much more serious reasons for suicide.

* * *

I chose an easier way – I decided not to leave my apartment any more. If I was destined to be alone, then I really shall be. Just as generals sacrifice the infantry, so I gave away the whole outside world in order to keep my honour. I shut myself in my room, because only there could I keep the remainder of my pride. The thin walls of the new building protected me from the remainder of the town. But, not for one moment did I consider going away.

Quite simply, I didn't have the strength for a new life. Besides which, I couldn't imagine that it would be any better for me anywhere else. Why would some different town be kinder towards me?9 Fully convinced of that fact, I stayed for nine months and three days in bed.

That was how it was... I hope it's now somewhat clearer how momentous, difficult and stressful my renewed encounter with the town was for me. There I was, walking bundled up in my coat and scarf through the dead of night. It was past midnight: infrequent voices echoed, footsteps crunched on the snow, a train in the distance murmured dully like a waterfall. I heard one young man saying confidingly to his friend, 'And I was so happy I peeled like an orange'. I saw the night watchman dozing in his kiosk, under a calendar filled with pictures of penguins. I came across a girl with a white fur cap on her head who was talking to a Mercedes. I heard the homeless people in their manholes talking in their sleep. I walked quickly, so that no-one would think I was just out for a stroll. I wanted it to look like I was returning from work, from a night shift, that I was hurrying home where chicken soup and a warm family were waiting for me.10

All at once I found myself in front of the Music School. I certainly hadn't intended to end up there, I am sure of that, and it wasn't a question of habit either, for I seldom walked that way. Without understanding how it happened, I suddenly found myself there, as though I had been teleported, put down in the school yard. The building at that time looked like the kind of House of Horrors Tim Burton would design. A damaged street light flashed every few seconds, throwing the shadows of a poplar tree across the façade, as if it was drawing the building's blood. The wind was screaming like an over-full vacuum cleaner. By day, the school was tame, even merry, coloured blue, which harmonized nicely with the orange façade of the day-care centre across the road. On one window of the kindergarten a sun made of gold paper was shining. I imagined the guard watching from the entrance the children at play, smoking his cigarette and twirling his keys around his fingers while his colleagues in the basement beat up the prisoners. A very possible picture, and not at all exaggerated. I had seen many similar, desperately disproportionate and unpleasant contrasts during the war.[11] I found them very hard to endure...

I returned home, tired. Sitting on the chair, I thought about how I could help Mirna but failed to think of anything. I had no sort of influence in the town, and I didn't even know anyone who had.[12]

And then my headache arrived. It did not behave as it had led me to expect – with pressure in my eyes and the skin on my forehead stretching. The pain came like a blow and stayed like that, just as powerful. I turned on the light and tried to find some kind of tablet to lessen the pain. But without success; it had been a long time since my apartment contained anything capable of helping me.

I lay awake all night. I can't remember what I was doing in the morning when Mirna came; most probably drinking coffee and pretending to wake myself up.[13]

From the door she said, 'You have to help me.' And then quickly added, 'Please.'

My thoughts incoherent from sleeplessness, I asked, 'What happened?'

'Today we have to go to the apartment.'

She walked two steps ahead of me. She hadn't wanted to wait for me to tie my shoelaces, so snow was leaking into my shoes. We moved along beside the wall of the big prison, situated almost in the centre of town. From the top of the square watch tower a guard was observing us. Presumably he should have been looking inside, and not outside. Who was he guarding? When Mirna stopped all at once in front of a building, I nearly walked into her. She lifted her head towards the windows. Like Mustafa.

'That's where you were living?' I asked.

'Aha, on the third floor.'

'So, shall we?'

'I can't, you have to understand. It's hard for me; I can't bear the thought that strangers are living in my apartment. I had a nightmare like that in my childhood. I dreamt I woke up in the morning, and mum and dad weren't there with me, instead there were some completely unknown people. After dreams like that, I used not to open my eyes because I was afraid it was still happening. You go by yourself, say you're a cousin, whatever you like. But, please, see who is in there. I'll wait for you here.'

What could I do? She was persuasive, and I was confused. In front of the building, bundled up in big thick jumpers and crowned with even bigger woollen caps, two women were sitting on small wooden stools, knitting. During the war people had started to sit in front of their lobbies, either from fear or from necessity in order to keep one another under surveillance. I had thought that habit had ended after the peace accord, but obviously these two old women didn't want to stop their companionship. I had to pass between them in order to go into the building. With one accord they lifted their heads from their knitting and looked me up and down, quickly but thoroughly.

The lift was not working, I walked up to the third floor and found the door on which was written *Aleksa Ranković*. The once-white door was completely dirty, covered with a disgusting scum like a scab on a wound. I pressed the door bell, but it didn't work. I decided to knock, clenched my teeth and quickly hit the wood twice with my fist. The sound was dull, as though the door was upholstered or even, if that is not too far-fetched a thought, as though I was hitting the back of some large animal. There was no answer. I went closer to the door, and pricked my ears. Silence. But this was not a normal silence. This was inhabited. Something was living in it. It had composed itself and was holding its breath. I cannot explain, but that is what I felt – something, full of anger, hatred. That it was alive, but also dead, at the same time. It seems difficult to understand, but that is truly what I felt. And I was certain I was not mistaken. I wanted to knock once more, made my fingers into a fist, lifted up my hand, came close to the door. But straight away I let my hand fall and hid it behind my back. I was afraid my fist would sink into the board and that that thing from the silence on the other side would grab it. The horror of this thought was magnified by a sudden darkness in the vestibule. That is not an unusual happening, and there was no magic involved, just the timing-out of the automatic light switch. Yet, this explanation did not calm me at all. The darkness was appalling. It pressed down on me like thousands of wet, plush curtains. It smelt of dampness, of some terrible illness, or the squat toilets at old railway stations. With my hands I searched the walls, slapped them with my palms, looking for that switch; but it was nowhere. I could take no more. I rushed down the stairs, slipped down the banisters, banged into the walls and came to a stop exactly in front of the two old women on their stools. From one of the woollen heaps a voice broke the silence:

'What's chasing you, dear child?'

I murmured some kind of greeting in response, pulled my head between my shoulders and ran off around the corner of the building.

Mirna was standing next to a perfectly executed snowman.

'And?' she asked with a lovely smile.

'There's nobody,' I answered, trying to catch my breath.

She cooled her forehead on the snowman's cheek.

'What do you mean nobody?' The smile had disappeared completely, as though wiped away.

'Fine and dandy. The doorbell doesn't work, I knocked twice, and no-one appeared.'

'Promise me you'll try again tomorrow,' she said, taking me by the hand.

I hoped she wouldn't notice the sweat on my palm.

'I will, no worries,' I promised.

'Then I'll see you again,' she freed my hand and started off down the street.

'Where?' I shouted after her.

'At the same time, next to the snowman.'

Fuck the snowman. I hoped the sun would finally come out tomorrow and melt it. But there didn't seem much chance of that, for the sky was a grey, metallic colour and it seemed completely impermeable, so that even the sun couldn't get through it. An icy wind was drying the snow, turning it into dust, picking it up, twisting it around and throwing it into people's eyes. Passers-by were walking quickly, heads lowered, to avoid the cold crystals. The town was depressing, sleepy and hung-over. At midday. I thought how I hadn't actually missed much in nine months. And three days.

At that point, I decided to start the search at the town radio station. A logical decision, you will agree. Aleksa spent a lot of time on the radio. And so did I, once upon a time...[14]

Desolation met me at the radio station. At reception there was an empty coffee cup, in the office the only things moving were the screen savers on the computers, in the studio WinAmp was changing MP3s by itself. Like in those post-apocalyptic films. But I knew that Mirza would have managed to survive even the end of the world. I found him in his office, a little room full of old radios, tape recorders, gramophones, televisions, vacuum cleaners, irons and some very hard to recognise equipment which had been waiting decades to be repaired. Cables were hanging from the ceiling, and he was pushing his way through them in his white clogs. Mirza is the oldest worker at the radio station; he claims to be one of the founders, although he retracts that statement as soon as someone mentions pensions. Because of his time-honoured status he thought he had ownership rights to the firm. He is known by the quite serious claim that without him there would be no programme.

'Until I lift up the regulator, nothing goes to air!'

When technological advances finally arrived at the town radio station, Mirza was shocked at the introduction of a DJ show in which the young men controlled the programming and worked at the mixing desk at the same time. He never adopted digital technology, and management kept him at his job only because he disciplined the new technicians and reported everything, even the least little oversight, in an orderly manner. Because of his extraordinary stubbornness and equally impressive short temper, the journalists didn't like to work with Mirza. However, Aleksa assembled all his reports with him and used to say that there was no greater master of the tape recorder than he was. In return, Aleksa was the only journalist Mirza respected.

'What was Aleksa like before his departure? Did you notice anything unusual?' I asked him.

He wound a thick wire around his elbow, gloomy and concentrated.

'He was never the same man after the war started. He withdrew into himself, kept quiet. I told him to wake up, that we needed professional people in those hard times. He only answered 'well I'm here, if anyone needs anything' and went off to the mine. Fuck that mine.'

'And, the day before he left?'

'Nothing. Well, actually there is something, I was keeping it...'

He put a large notebook on the table, with the title *Observation Book of the Journalist on Duty*.

'You remember, when radio was truly radio, journalists used to write such things. Even in the war there was order, and see this now... Yes, Aleksa was orderly... He wrote down his last working day as well... He's a serious man. Everything is in there...'

I began to turn over the pages of the notebook, but he shut it with his palm. I thought he was going to begin with his stories about how order must exist and that the notebook could not be read by unauthorised people, but he said:

'OK, take it home, no-one needs this sort of thing here anymore. But, more important, tell me, has he contacted you?'

I did not know what to tell him, so just said, 'No, but his daughter came back...'

He interrupted me, 'I didn't expect that from him. There were all sorts of deserters, they left in silence, then afterwards talked against us. But, I didn't expect that from Aleksa. At least he could have contacted me, we were good friends - the two of us were the station...'

I waited for him to lift his hand from the notebook so I could leave.

'Tell his daughter to say to him that Mirza is angry with him. Don't forget... Go now, I'm busy, someone has to work around here.'

He unwound the wire and immediately started to wind it up again. I went out into the corridor, and he remarked after me:

'Don't keep that notebook too long. We must maintain some sort of order.'

I hurried home, almost running. I slipped a few times, but even so I managed to get the notebook into my apartment in one piece. Still in my coat and with my cap on my head, I sat down at the table and opened it. Straight away it could be seen that Aleksa had been the most hardworking commentator in it, always polite and measured.

For instance, on 25th May 1993 he had noted down:

In the main information broadcast I would single out the contribution of colleague S. M. about the spring action to clean up the town. Our young colleague succeeded in finding a fresh approach to an old theme. Congratulations.

A contribution in the news of the 30 May had not appealed to him.

The conversation with the president of the non-governmental organization Together in Crisis was tiring, totally confusing and nonsensical.

Our good Aleksa then continued with the addition:

I believe we do not need to blame our colleague because of this. We can see clearly by his questions that he had prepared himself well for this conversation, but the other speaker obviously does not know what his organisation really deals with. In the conversation he was using scientific phrases in the wrong places.

Aleksa's colleagues were not so responsible in their observations. The commentary on the news of 2nd June was:

Mirela, I love you!

The journalist on duty had commented on the program for the 6th of June like this:

I left two slices of bread for you in the cupboard with the cassettes. That brown stuff in the paper is lentil paste.

A few pages were full of short lines from a card game, as well as simple mathematical transactions, and in large letters there was the existential wail:

Does anyone know when we will be paid? Or at least, cigarettes?

Near the end of the notebook I found Aleksa's last message, written on the 2nd of August 1993. He wrote, in his orderly, composed handwriting:

I am sorry to be saying goodbye to you in this way, my dear colleagues, but it is the only way possible. Believe me when I say that this is not my choice and that I am bound by the demands of others. I hope you will understand me. If not, the day will come when I shall apologise to you in person and explain the problem. If I may, I would like to recommend:
    Mirza can take the Uher and decide to whom he will give it.

It is a sensitive instrument and there is a problem with the microphone cable so it should be handled very carefully. I am also asking Mirza to make sure the vinyl singles are upright when put away, also the LPs. If they keep getting put one on top of the other, the grooves will be worn down. Also, I would like some young journalist to take jurisdiction over the mining industry for himself. I think the theme of the open-cut mines has still enough potential for a detailed analysis.

That's all for now, until we meet again, soon.

Regards to you all from your Aleksa.

And that was all. That was the last entry in the notebook; it looked as though Mirza had taken it out of the office. That was not enough for me to escape an encounter with the door. I had to continue with the search. To find something to make Mirna happy, some information to shed some light on Aleksa's secret. I looked through the window and it suddenly occurred to me. In fact, it wasn't so hard. The continuation of the story was unfolding before my eyes.

* * *

The Ant, as the miners called him, or Vernes in normal life, lived on an estate I could see every day from the chair in my kitchen. It was a small group of low houses, the eaves almost touching the ground. It was said that they were built on top of old mine tunnels, or else the tunnels were tucked underneath them; it was hard to say what came first, but either way it meant the settlement could easily sink into the earth. Every year the town authorities announce that they will destroy it, but quickly change their minds when they remember they have to offer the tenants new accommodation. And so the little houses have been creaking in the weakest of winds for years, squeezed between garages and the marketplace wall. Regardless of this lack of space, the owners try obstinately to make them bigger. They have extended the narrow rooms, opened low doors, put in little windows, dug out cellars, put up narrow terraces, and joined it all together with steep staircases and small roofs. After all these prodigious adaptations, if this word can be used to describe them, the houses have completely lost their original shape, and are now crooked, shifted from their foundations and merged with one another. Some of the doors in this settlement do not match human dimensions, and there are windows where there are no rooms to be aired. Looking at them now, it seemed as though they had shot up through the earth by themselves, that their illogically-placed roofs were actually just the tips of some big buildings extending under the earth.

I met the Ant when I was working as a journalist and he was the president of the Union. He was not surprised when I went to visit him. When I asked him if he could answer a few questions for me, he said:

'What the fuck is wrong with you, I'm retired.'

I lied that I was writing a text about former miners. He agreed, maybe out of boredom.

I had to bend my head in the doorway, step over a high threshold and down onto a creaking floor which swayed beneath our feet. A calendar from 1983 with a photo of Biljana Jevtić, dressed as Kim Wilde, covered a big crack which distorted the wall behind a portable television. You could have pushed a few pencils through the crack, if not something fatter.

We sat on armchairs, while between us was a low table. These things, together with posters of singers, a cupboard and the television, were the only objects to be found in the little room.

'I don't drink either alcohol or coffee and I don't smoke, since I retired. I can offer you biscuits and water, if you're inclined.'

From the small cupboard he pulled out a packet of tea biscuits which we bit into together. We kept silent, chewing and brushing the crumbs from our collars every now and then, until it was time for the interview, which, if we're being honest, I hadn't surpassed even at 'the height of my career'.

'How much is your pension?'

'Two hundred and eighty Deutschmarks.'

'Can you make ends meet?'

'We've put up with worse.'

'How was it working in the mines when you were a young miner?'

'Like it is now, with a shovel.'

'The best memory from your mining days?'

'The comradeship of my colleagues.'

'A day you will never forget?'

'When I brought out my dead comrades.'

'What advice would you give to young miners?'

'Good luck.'

'Can we get into Europe with mines like these?'

'We can't go anywhere.'

'Do you have anything to say to our readers?'

'No, I haven't.'

I folded up the paper on which I had written down his answers, which meant that the official part of the conversation was finished, so the Ant threw a biscuit into his mouth.

I asked him if he remembered Aleksa.

'How would I not remember him? During the war he used to bring me that black Dutch tobacco. I've never smoked anything so fine.' He closed his little black eyes.

He opened them when I asked him what they talked about.

'He wanted me to tell him about the unusual things I had seen in the pit. I had nothing to tell him... I close my eyes before I go into the pit, like a chauffeur in front of a tunnel, and it seems to me I open them only when I go out again. Now when I think about it, it's as though I never opened them during the war. It's all in some sort of darkness.'

'Why did you forbid him to go down the mine?'

His high forehead went red and a few strands of hair stood on end. My legs were getting cold. The cold was coming through the floorboards.

'That's not true; I didn't let him go on the open cut.'

'Wasn't it shut then too?'

'Yes, but there were still open pits. And I was afraid of other things. Strange things had happened there.'

'What sort of strange things?'

The hairs on the top of his head moved, like little antennae.

'Terrible things.'

'What kind of things, tell me.'

'What can I tell you? What do you want me to say? Ugly, abnormal...'

'How were they abnormal?' I am not usually so persistent, but these were not normal circumstances.

'And what was normal during the war, fuck you? Tell me one normal thing!'

I thought of a few, I really did. For instance, during the war all we wanted was to survive. If that is not a normal need, then I don't know what is. After the war came those other things. That was the most important thing I thought of at that moment. The others were too personal. I had just decided to tell the Ant what I had thought of, when he slid off the armchair and said:

'Excuse me now, I have work to do. I might be retired, but I'm not just for fucking around.'

He saw me to the door and asked:

'And how is Aleksa? Give him my regards when you see him. Tell him I still remember that tobacco.'

'I will, as soon as I see him.'

This visit wasn't enough to satisfy Mirna, either. I realised I had to prepare myself well for another new day and that the most important thing to concentrate on was a good night's sleep.

I changed the bedclothes, had a shower, put on clean pyjamas, drank camomile tea and lay down. But as soon as I touched the bed, I knew I would not be able to fall asleep. I remember turning off the light, but the darkness did not embrace me, the room did not become a pleasant box. It became wider, ten times bigger, turned into a horrible emptiness: the steppe, the tundra, something cold like that, vast and yet full of anxiety. Or, to describe it better, it turned into the plains of Vojvodina in autumn. I was there, so I know what it's like. I began to prick up my ears in the room, listening for the slightest sound, and driving away sleep. I got up, picked up a book, one I had read a long time ago with pleasure, which would not upset me, whose sentences should be only pleasant, calming... I can't remember which, but that's not important, because it didn't help; anxiety was buzzing around the apartment and feeding my insomnia. Inevitably, I soon returned to analysing the happenings which had led to my being left alone. I tried to recall the conversations and searched for the beginning of the breakdown, and remembered one evening, while I was studying the television guide, when she said, 'I am sure you do not love me as much as I love you.'

I was not in the mood for this type of conversation, being absorbed in reading the condensed contents of the evening's films in the TV guide.[15] She repeated the sentence, with the same tone, I recall. I understood that I still had to answer.

'How do you mean?'

'Just as I said. I simply do not believe you love me.'

'So, what can I do now? How can I convince you?'

'That isn't my problem,' she said, and took the remote control.

The conversation was ended like that; I went back to the television guide, and she... I don't remember.

Even now I am not exactly sure what I should have answered or done. But, I should have done something. In one film, I forget its title, Mickey Rourke hugs a blind girl. She tells him she would be very happy if she could see his face. Mickey thinks for a short while, takes the lamp from the little cupboard and brings it up to his face. I should have done something like that. Anything. Better than nothing.

I lay awake all night. But I do remember one dream, because somehow the morning brought me memories of it. That made me conclude I had fallen asleep after all, not much, but just enough for a little nightmare.

Once again, I dreamt of the man with the big eyes. I only saw his face, leaning on the highest window of the Music School.

His lips were moving. The words coming out of his mouth were making varying patterns of steam on the window. I stood in the school yard and shouted: 'Mustafa has spoken: It is not my fault!' In the orange sky a sun of golden paper was shining. Its rays were drilling holes into my shoulders.

I had been dreaming, for what else could have happened?

I had not left the bedroom. The place looked terrible, as though the insomnia had remained in it and blown it full of poisonous gases. The sheets on the bed were chewed up, the pillows smelled awful. They say that the sweat of a madman has an especially strong smell. Mine smelt like bad potatoes.

Later I went into the lounge and saw the tracks of muddy shoes on the floor. They were quite clear, like the marks of dancing steps. I noticed two pairs of footsteps. One was small, from an owner who had worn pointed shoes. The other muddy footprints were left by big shoes with a rounded top. They covered the whole room, and it was easy to follow them and see how they had stopped before the shelves, the pictures, the drawers... One could conclude what they had looked at, what had interested them... But I didn't have the time to think about it. Mirna was waiting for me.

Looking through the window, I saw that nothing had changed outside. The snowman was still standing in his place, solid and strong, like the steel sky above him. A flock of tame pigeons took flight from the rooftop. They made a sharp formation and darted up into the heights, but broke into unruliness after a few dozen metres, as though they had flown into a wall.

I decided not to meet up with Mirna. After such a night, I was not ready for any further effort. I planned to tell her I hadn't been able to, had been ill, I would think of something...[16] I often used various ways of getting out of obligations, but this time I really had a good excuse to give up, I had had a sleepless night, I was tired... I promised myself that tomorrow, as soon as I felt stronger; I would knock again on the door of Aleksa's apartment.

My eyes were burning from sleeplessness, and nausea was

crouching in my stomach. I was weak, my whole body was shaking, I was disappearing like a lolly on the tongue... to treat myself to a sweet comparison. I felt I could not confront that door again in such a weak state, much less what awaited me behind it. Instead, I had to go shopping, to get food, and strength. I had nothing edible left in the flat.

I don't like visiting shops, particularly not supermarkets, which look to me as though they were made from Lego blocks. People wander around the shelves like tourists, admiring the packaging created according to an average conception of beauty; choosing products shining like jewels, full of colour like rare algae in *National Geographic*, holding contents into which it is a sin to sink your teeth, breaking them into pieces and letting them slide down the sticky horror of the digestive tract. People turn objects over in their hands, read the instructions, the advertising messages, discuss the contents, the double packaging, the 'best before' date, vitamin content, emulsifiers, artificial flavours, preservatives, acidity. They confer with their partners, with other buyers, seek advice from shop attendants and then listen distrustfully. They put the things they have chosen into their baskets several times, take them out again, compare them with something similar, put them back or change them, then go to the check-out never quite sure they have made the right choice. I, luckily, have no problem with indecisiveness. I had decided to eat uniform food, so as to reduce the number of daily decisions, and therefore lower the level of stress. I have chosen tea biscuits as my staple meal. I have been eating them for months. I've got used to them, and just the thought of any other food causes nausea to rise in my stomach. Wolves eat only meat, and cows eat nothing but grass and they feel perfectly all right.[17]

With packets of biscuits in my pocket I left the labyrinth of shelves and went to visit Ahmed.

'Old rabbis used to say that a person who does not fear the glory of his Maker and who searches for that which is above, that which is below, that which is in front and that which is behind, would be better off never seeing the light of day.' I am sure I have remembered this sentence of Ahmed's accurately. Because then, for the first time, it occurred to me that something dreadful had happened to Aleksa.

I found Ahmed in his office; a small room hidden in the corner of the library. I had met him while I was working as a journalist, but even that superficial acquaintance was enough for him to greet me warmly. He offered me a worn chair. On the table between us lay a small set of magnetic chess. I could see that the figures on the board were in the middle of a game, but I didn't understand the positions, or who was winning the duel. I have never learnt how to play chess, and knew only which way the figures moved. Yet people often ask me to play, probably from a need to prove themselves. Ahmed's office was neat and modest. He poured some really good herbal brandy, which smelt like an intoxicating island –full of ikebana. Into his own glass he poured first water, then only a few drops of the brandy.

'I can't drink because of my liver. At least I can taste a little bit like this,' he explained.

It was pleasant, and I felt a sleepiness come over me. And then I saw the picture.

It was hanging on the wall above Ahmed's head. It was old; the oil colours had long ago lost their sheen. A thin horse was painted on the canvas, in the way Đorđe Andrejević Kun used to paint. This horse didn't have a typhus sufferer on his back, he was standing alone in the darkness, his dull eyes could only just be seen in the gloom. My mouth became completely dry when I understood: it was a blind horse from the mines, a pitiful animal which thinks the world is a dark tunnel.

Ahmed was looking at me so I had to compose myself quickly. He looked like Aleksa. Maybe friends, like husbands and wives or dogs and their masters, begin to look like one another when they are together for a long time. With the thumb of one hand he was caressing the top of a tiny chess queen, and with the other he slowly circled the edge of the glass.

I told him Mirna had returned to town and was asking about her father.

He sighed so deeply that the air in the room was disturbed.

'So, now it's perfectly clear, Aleksa is not with them,' he whispered sadly.

I just nodded my head.

'I knew it, he would have contacted me. I'd like to see Mirna, where is she?'

I wanted to answer him, but I realised only then that I did not know where Mirna was. She had always come to me.

'She's here, in town,' I whispered.

After that, we fell silent. I sobered up from the effects of the brandy and wondered what to do next. Then I said, just by the way, 'She gave me Aleksa's diary. '

Ahmed's finger lifted from the queen's head. I added, 'I know you were looking for Perkman.'

He got up from the chair. He was a head taller than I.

'Do you know what Perkman is?' he asked me.

'Yes, I know,' I answered as steadily as I could; trying to withstand his gaze even though I felt an itch between my eyebrows.

'But you never saw him?' He was serious, I remember, even dramatic.

'No I haven't, but I will see him.' I was serious too.

It was as though this answer calmed him. He sat down, lowered his head and stared at the chess board. When he looked at me again, he had a smile on his face that I can only describe now as 'Pre-Perkman'. He got up from the chair and went over to the metal filing cabinet. Theatrically, he pronounced:

'I believe in the existence of worlds which are more exalted than ours and in the existence of beings that inhabit these worlds. I believe we can, depending on the level of our spiritual harmony, communicate with higher beings.'

Only after these words, which, without knowing their origin, I interpreted then as an oath,[18] did he unlock the cupboard and begin to take out some white folders. He stacked at least fifty of them carefully on the table.

Over this paper wall, with obvious pride, he told me that in

71

the folders were listed all the demons, ghosts, spirits, vampires, werewolves, witches, fairies and similar beings that had appeared in Bosnia-Herzegovina over the past fifty years. Amongst them was noted the case of the 'House of Ghosts', the ruins above the train station in Doboj, where Ahmed had spent the night while the rest of the human race was celebrating entering the 21st century. In the files were descriptions of all the fights of the unearthly strongmen on the white wall at Nemila, the appearance of giants at Gradačac and Listica, the Roman spirit Puhala at Tuzla (if I remember correctly), the apparition of sleepers from the tomb at Vranduk, the conversion of godless Lutherans from Žepa. Here too were his own stories of vampire hunters from Krajina, with whom he had stayed during the winter of 1968. In another file, he dealt with the legend of Jure Grando, the vampire from Kriga, whose case he researched during a summer holiday in Istria. He spoke quickly; there was more, but I can't remember everything. For the first time in my life, I was listening to a truly fascinating story and I didn't have a Dictaphone.

'I've been collecting these stories all my life,' he said calmly, then widened his eyes and roared, 'but never, not even once have I ever seen anything! What makes you think you are better than I am?'

I kept quiet; I felt guilty, as though I had told a terrible lie. But then I added, 'Who are Jedžudž and Medžudž? '

Ahmed sat in the chair and thought quickly. I saw him bite his lip. All at once he got up, grabbed his coat and went towards the door:

'We'll talk somewhere else.'

The old man was shuffling along in front of me, and I followed him, staggering on the icy footpath, crumpled and drowsy. There was no-one on the street, the town hummed around us like a machine in wait mode. Finally, we went into a small cafe; a place I had never noticed before even though I had been going down that street for years. It was attractive, covered with thick carpet, with an old wooden bar, heavy plush curtains, upholstered chairs, photographs in oval frames (they were portraits, but I didn't notice whose), racks for newspapers. A thin waiter in a red waistcoat with black lapels danced over to us with a napkin draped over his arm and an eyebrow raised. He served us the same brandy we had been drinking in the library. I felt that this was a place I could relax in. It seemed to me that all at once time had slowed down, without my understanding how and why.

'Do you know who the Pegasus brothers are?' he asked me as soon as the waiter had glided away to the bar.

Of course I knew. The whole town knew about them.

* * *

The story of the Pegasus brothers

In a little settlement near the steel factory lived Adem and Badema Pegasus. Adem was a large, sullen lathe operator who seldom smiled. He spoke even more rarely, so it was hard to say much more about him. His wife Badema was absolutely beautiful, constructed in perfect proportions and with the most harmonious arrangement of facial features. Nobody ever found out from whence Adem had brought her, but when she went out into the yard for the first time, the news of her sensational beauty flowed with previously unheard-of speed through all the little houses. On the dusty track in front of the Pegasus home, there was a march-past of all the families in the settlement in order to look her up and down from head to toe and store the picture in their memories, to beautify their sad days. She was the point where the erotic fantasies of the inhabitants of the settlement intersected, more beautiful than any of the television hostesses, more alluring than the Lotto girls and more radiant than the beauties on chocolate boxes. In between the bathtubs full of holes, orange water-heaters, poison weeds, old car tyres, tinned cabbage, plastic dwarfs and similar objects from the settlement's set design; she walked with a touching elegance and pride. When she threw back her heavy, black hair, and the sun found all possible colours in it, you could have wept and smiled at the same time from such beauty. The unpremeditated, promise-filled sound of her laughter or the completely unintentional curving of her body provoked explosive wet dreams in young men, and husbands gnashed their teeth. All the older women very quickly grew to hate her and hissed with gossip as she passed by, and little girls followed her in groups and mimicked her movements. Badema did not notice this attention or, more likely, she pretended not to see it. She seldom went out; the neighbours mostly saw her washing the black dust off the flowers in her yard, or waiting at the window for her husband to return from the factory. And she was always alone...

Still, Adem was jealous; he was afraid of losing his beauty and was always sniffing out the tracks of possible intruders. He would come home at different times from his job, open the front door with a bang, and still in his shoes and coat, he would search the room. He was also seen spying on the house from the bushes and crawling under the window. They say he laughed for the first time in his life when he heard that Badema was pregnant, and for a whole three days he toasted the silhouettes of the factory when he learnt that there were twins lying in her stomach. He called them Albin and Aldin, he adored them, he would almost run through the settlement when he returned home from work, and once he even hung the nappies himself on the line in the yard. They were a beautiful family, the adornment of the whole settlement.

The tragedy began with the first white locks on the children's heads. Until then, all the Pegases had been black-haired, so their father immediately concluded the children could not on any account be his. His neighbours tried to calm him down, told him that often happened, and that their hair would darken as soon as they started to walk.

'If the children's hair does not go black then.' said Adem to Badema, 'you will turn blue.'

In anticipation of their first steps, the father calmed his nerves with grape brandy. As the boys grew, his anxiety grew too, and with it a greater and greater need for alcohol. One evening, the brothers held one another's hands, unsteadily got up from the floor and slowly went over to their father, who was watching television. While they were swaying on the balls of their little feet, the white curls danced on their heads. Adem pushed them backwards onto the floor; they fell with a scream, like rubber toys. That evening he beat Badema for the first time... After that, he beat her every day, without exception. To lessen his anger, Badema cropped the boys' hair to their scalps, but the father easily discerned the white fluff and then beat her even more. When at sunset the settlement became quiet and families sat down to eat their evening meal, her cries announced the coming of the night; and they stopped around midnight, when Adem had no strength left. No-one from the settlement even tried to help the poor woman. The men thought it would be a dangerous precedent to entangle themselves in marital affairs not their own, and the women thought there was some justice in it, because her beauty had been unfair towards them. After a short time, the neighbours had become quite used to Badema's cries, just as they accepted the daily earth shattering blows of the heavy metallurgy from the factory.

The boys grew, as white as the clothes in advertisements for washing powder. They were always alone; Badema spent the days recovering from her beatings, and the other children avoided them, according to the orders of their mothers. The twins roamed between the houses like little ghosts and thought up games of their own. They learnt anatomy by taking out the innards of live frogs, researched aerodynamics by pulling out the wings of sparrows, examined the threshold of pain while they set light to cats they had tied up, and threw stones at dogs... They liked to watch how life went out of the eyes of animals and compete to see who would be first to notice the coming of death.

Animals ran away from them, and they in turn avoided people. The neighbours too pretended not to see them, until things began to disappear in the settlement – bicycles, clothes, pies from windowsills, hard fruit from the trees, slippers from in front of doors, tools forgotten in the grass... The settlement did not think about it for too long, for everyone concluded that the brothers Pegasus were the culprits, and decided to solve the problem inside the local co-operative. At that meeting (which had never had a greater attendance), following a debate on the dynamics of rubbish collection, under the item of 'current matters' they discussed ways to 'bring the boys to their senses'.

It was dusk when the local people prepared an ambush. They waited for the twins in a dark, blind alley, surrounded them and hit them with lathes, sticks, army belts, rolling-pins – whatever they could find in their houses. The boys' cries mixed with Badema's, who twenty metres or so further on was enduring Adem's blows. The beating stopped when the boys lost consciousness, but there was still strength in the punishment group; they were all strong grown men, metalworkers, they could have kept beating them until morning; but it was no longer interesting, the lesson was finished. They parted cheerfully, chatting, walking off with their weapons across their shoulders, like peasants returning from reaping. Behind them, in the black dust, in the shallow dark of nightfall, two small bodies remained lying.

The boys somehow got themselves home and no-one saw them for nearly a year. No-one knows how they recovered from the beating. But everyone remembers the morning when they came out again into the light of day. Quite unmoving, they stood in the doorway, in the square of shade coming out from the house. Some say they stood like that for ten minutes, others swear it was half an hour, and there are those who stubbornly repeat that the Pegasus brothers stood there for a whole hour. That is not even important, what is important is that at the same time, surely completely pre-arranged, they took one step forward, left the darkness and stood in the sunlight. The light reflected from their heads. They had completely red hair! But, the colour of their hair was no longer of great consequence; black or white did not matter in this case. Adem had been given a long sentence for the murder of his wife, and Badema lay under a wooden grave-marker in the cemetery on the hill above the factory. The boys squinted in the sun for a few minutes, and when they strode out into the street, everyone in the settlement closed their windows and doors. While they walked slowly, everything with a heart became quiet and still. Only the transistor radios could be heard playing the usual folk songs from the windows. That morning the worst criminals in the town's history were born.

Albin is burly, constructed like a concrete dam, with enormous fists and a fat neck. Aldin grew out into a flat thin man with narrow shoulders and thin hands. They both have wide faces on which there is room for another pair of eyes. Their own eyes are small; Albin's are shiny and restless; whereas sharks have eyes similar to Aldin's – empty and cold over which a transparent eyelid slips like a shark's as soon as he opens his small, sharp-toothed mouth.

Perhaps Albin is not the strongest man in town, but everyone knows he never forgets. Anyone who fights with him knows he had better make an end of him immediately, because Albin will certainly come back to finish what he started. They say that in his whole life Aldin never loved anything or anyone. He puts up only with Albin, and even that is only from habit. It is said they love to torture people and that they now behave towards people as they previously did towards animals. That they have brought their science of death to perfection so that they can keep victims for days on the brink between two worlds and then at the last moment bring them back. Into this world. Or push them forward. Whatever they please...

Stories like this have enabled the Pegasus brothers to keep the whole town under control without any trouble at all. All the town's shopkeepers and traders bring them a percentage of their earnings and would rather shut their business than try to lessen their contribution. The police turn a blind eye to their reign of terror, because the Pegases control the under-ground world too. They always keep to the same level of criminal activity, they do not allow any increase which would worry the authorities and force the police into action. Nothing can happen without their knowledge. Every criminal, down to the least important pickpocket, has to get permission from them to work, and give them a portion of the plunder. They have both the criminals and the police in their hands, justice and injustice. They alone determine the centre between light and dark. They create dusk.

* * *

'Aleksa was seen several times in the company of the Pegases,' said Ahmed softly, coughing, and then adding even more softly, 'you know yourself that they used to get people out of town during the war, people who had the money to pay for it. I think Aleksa must have approached them too.'

I just couldn't imagine Aleksa talking with the Pegases. They did not belong to the same world.

'You have to know that, after he met Perkman, Aleksa was not the same man. He believed he had to see the spirit again and listen to his message. He thought that that was an extremely important task, truly a mission. And because of that he assumed, I am sure, that nothing could happen to him until he carried out this task. He nearly got me believing it too... Nothing could change his mind, no matter how much we talked about it.'

Ahmed did not say, but I knew, that he was afraid the curse of the rabbi might be fulfilled, because he added, 'It wasn't so terrible that he was an atheist, it's terrible that until that encounter he didn't believe in spirits either. The spirits don't forgive unbelievers; I'm surprised he succeeded in surviving the first encounter.'

He explained to me that Aleksa had approached his investigation as though he were puzzling out a treasure map. That he didn't take anything especially seriously.

'That's the reason he accepted the Pegases so easily. He was not interested in who they were, as long as he could get to his goal through their help. They promised that they would make possible the two most important meetings for him – with Perkman and with Anđela and Mirna. He even started to believe that they were the twins from the prediction.'

'So, he went off with the Pegases?'

The old man nodded his head.

'Does that mean...?'

He hit the table with his open hand, not letting me finish the sentence. He knew what my response would be. People were saying that the Pegases had caused the biggest number of missing people during the war. Really missing. Nobody, ever, even if he had been brave enough, had been able to accuse them of murder, because not one body was ever found. The waiter came up to the table with a new glass of brandy. One swallow helped me to look at the problem a bit more realistically. The war had ended long ago, there was a country now; miserable and unsteady, but still it existed...

'I'll report everything to the police,' I said.

I asked Ahmed if he would be a witness. He looked at me, a little bit derisorily.

'I will, but all I can tell them are stories about spirits.'

I got up from the chair, almost jumping; the waiter came up to me, helped me put on my coat and saw me to the door.

'I hope you will come here again. You will be a welcome guest. Ahmed will wait for you here, at the same table.' The waiter's smile showed all his teeth, which were unnaturally symmetrical.

I turned around. In the whole room, with its ten imposing tables, in the warm silence, the soft half-darkness, Ahmed was the only guest.[19] He sat stoop-shouldered right in the centre of the bar. The low lamp hanging from the ceiling circled the table with a gentle light. Like in a monodrama.

* * *

Outside, it was the dead of night.[20] I couldn't believe I had been so long in the bar. I once read that one of the signs of the coming of Judgement Day would be a speeding up of the passage of time. Muslims believe the Prophet said that Judgement Day will not come about until time passes very quickly, so that a year will pass like a month, a month like a week, a week like a day, and an hour will be as long as the time it takes to burn one palm leaf.

Judging by the small number of lit windows, I presumed it was past midnight. I staggered along the streets, weak from excitement, fatigue, slippery footpaths, countless glasses of brandy... A few passers-by slipped past, hurrying to get off the street, to go somewhere warm and safe. The night was not welcoming, it seemed to me that it made the shadows more deformed and the people disfigured.

I dragged myself up to the apartment building, unlocked the metal door and only just managed to open it. A very strong draught seemed to be opposing me. They say that a thick line of apartment buildings were built in the path of the wind and that changed the climate of the town. I don't know if that is true, but I do know that one side of the building is as cold as the grave even during the hottest weather.

I pressed the switch for the light and, as you can imagine, was very surprised when I saw Mustafa in front of the lift. He was staring at the list of 'House Rules' hanging on the wall. I was obliged to go past him. I thought he had not noticed me, but when I was one step away from him, all at once he turned, looked me directly in the eyes, hypnotically, like a snake with a mouse, and shouted:

'Tell him that you haven't slept for days!'

I was confused.

'What did you say?'

'Mustafa has spoken!' he concluded, and marched off away from the vestibule.

In the apartment, I tried to decipher Mustafa's message. This time it was certain that the message was meant only for me, but this knowledge did not help me to understand it. Only later would I understand and make good use of Mustafa's advice... We'll come to that in good time. Right now I should mention a different visitor, a new ringing at the door. After midnight, it sounded like an air-raid alert, ominous and full of panic.

Mirna was standing in the doorway, in the frame where I had already become used to seeing her. But the picture was quite different. She was not smiling this time, and that completely changed her face. She was angry, it was easy to see that – white skin, mouth pulled tight, eyes pressed down by her eyebrows...

'I've been waiting for you,' she whispered hoarsely.

'Sorry, I had an appointment, I can explain...'

'Maybe you can, but I can't listen, you promised and you lied.' She wasn't angry, she was furious.

She confused me, as I was not expecting such force. It was as though between us, from the sheer force of her fury, a minefield had grown. I remained silent. She calmly pronounced new orders.

'I'll wait for you tomorrow. Again. At the same place. At the same time.'

Even though I am on the seventh floor, she turned towards the steps.

'Wait, I'll call the lift for you.'

She did not answer, I heard only her heels tapping even faster. Maybe she thought her departure would not be dramatic enough if she waited for the lift.

I could not tell her what I had learnt from Ahmed. Not until I was sure.

While I was shutting the door I realised I would not be sleeping that night either. I did not suspect insomnia, at least not in the form to which I was accustomed. This feeling was quite new, something I had never experienced before. There was a strange intensity in my body, as though another person, a fresh person, one who had slept well and was full of energy, was trying to install himself in the same skin with me, to lean against my skeleton and to hitch on to my circulatory system. He had taken possession of my brain too; my thoughts were overlapping one another, I could not choose which one I needed to follow. Every noise reverberated like it does in a hall for physical training.

Everything had a rhythm, everything was looking for its partner. If I touched a glass I had to do it again, my small steps through the room had to be precise, all the same size and in a methodical rhythm. Not one movement could be carried out without my full concentration, and my co-inhabitor was the one making the decisions. If I did something incorrectly, if I made a mistake in the rhythm or resisted repeating a movement, he howled inside me, inside my skull a hot wind whirled, full of sharp dust. When I listened to him he laughed contentedly, but in a disgusting way, debauched; my eyes filled with tears because of his joy.

It occurred to me, with difficulty, while he obstructed me with orders to open the window, to measure the room by stepping diagonally, to shut the door of the fridge – all at the same time – that I would succeed in resisting him if I lay down, and tried not to move and not to think. But that too was not easy, my breathing imposed itself as an obligation and demanded that I speed up the rhythm, until it became a frenzied panting that was unbearable...

The morning found me stiff and alone. He left me, completely exhausted, with the first light. Without any announcement, just as he had arrived. All at once I felt that I was quite alone, that once again I could be in control. I was shivering, even though everything in me and on me was burning. I put on my coat, pulled my scarf tight around my wet neck and ran out of the apartment. Mirna was waiting for me...

* * *

I'm going to meet Mirna, I'll calm down on the way. I wasn't successful. Nausea was rising in my stomach. I tried to breathe through my nose to press it down, but I couldn't manage. My stomach heaved and pressed out a vile lump. It melted and softened in the cavity of my stomach, another contraction of my muscles resulted in, I presume, the whole mass spinning and forming into a geyser which found its way to my mouth. My neck straightened from the strength of the liquid, my jaws widened to let the torrent through, but nothing came out... There was no sign at all on the snow, and yet I felt a slight relief.

I reached the snowman. Mirna had not yet arrived; I decided to wait for her. I didn't know how long I would wait, and I could not even guess what the time was. All I knew was that the day had dawned. It seemed that today was visitors' day in the prison, for people with plastic bags were going through the gates – silent old people, pale women with noisy children, a few pretty women in fur coats...

'So you did come!' I heard Mirna's voice.

I turned around. She looked wonderful, truly dazzling, and that's not an empty phrase; she was the only colour on that grey day. You could not imagine a greater contrast between the three of us on the street – the dirty snowman, dazzling Mirna and crumpled me. I could not help the snowman, but I quickly smoothed my hair and cleaned the corners of my eyes. I tried to excuse my appearance.

'I slept really badly...'

She stopped me.

'We'll talk afterwards When you come back from the flat.'

An old man was coming out through the gates of the prison. He was laughing loudly and applauding. Mirna took no notice of him, just moved graciously to the side to allow him to get to the building. I was envious of the old man's hilarity; who could know what good news he had learnt inside? I don't think there was anyone in existence I did not envy at that moment, and both then and now, I could count a big number of things I would rather have done than stand again in front of that door. Among them; a visit to the dentist, an unfair fight, unexpected impotence, receiving a suspect doctor's report... Things like that...

'Get going, please.' She pushed me.

My stomach again became angry and made my steps even more unsure. In front of the lobby, those same women were sitting, at least the caps, scarves and jumpers were the same. They were not talking, they were joined together by the stitches they were knitting. I slipped through between their stares, like a burglar between laser beams; with a lot of help from the balustrade, I conquered the steps and stopped in front of that disgusting door. It looked as though the dirty scum on it was even thicker, for now it was exactly like the back of some reptile. My stomach was pulsating like a machine from hell when I banged with my fist on the door. It opened. On the other side darkness was waiting for me. *The Land of Oz is a wonderful place, but for me there are only places like this.*

I stepped forward and I remember thinking it was like going into a mine shaft. It took me a few moments for my eyes to get used to the dark. The walls were sooty, the parquet scratched, the remains of fire, cardboard boxes and newspapers covered the corners. The only piece of furniture in the flat, at least as far as I could see, was one chair, placed near the filthy window. It was being used by a man with huge eyes, exactly like the one from my dream. Wrapped in a black coat, he was sitting motionless, his back straight, like a yoga teacher. Even in such a weak light I could clearly see that the bloodshot eyes and thin mouth revealed a terrible anger which seemed to be growing every second. It seemed as though he would do something unimaginably awful when he could no longer endure the pressure of his anger.

Very quickly, I said, 'I haven't slept for days.'

I saw that the anger began to recede; in a video game, the barometer would have slipped down from the colour red.

I continued:

'I don't think I shall ever go to sleep again.'

He looked at me with curiosity, measured me from head to foot like an unusual object. His small mouth opened for a moment; and he spoke.

'How do you mean?'

'I don't know, but no matter how much I try, I can't sleep.'

'How do you manage that? I have to fight sleep all the time. I resist, but every seven days it strikes me down for at least half an hour.'

Calmly I informed him, 'I think something or someone exists that will not let me sleep. And that something is inside me.'

He got up from the chair and went to the window.

'The one who stops me from sleeping is lying in that building. I have to be awake when he comes out of jail.'

Suddenly, all at once, with no warning at all, no sort of announcement that would have prepared me, the scene was taken from in front of my eyes, the perspective changed, the view slanted unnaturally. As though I had entered a surrealist film, a black and white horror film. Some film director had taken over my life, was moving with his camera around the room, over the walls... I saw him for a moment, thin with red eyes, and then I saw myself – crazed, drained, sweaty, full of fear, fatigue, nausea, shock. After this striking take, the director fixed the camera on the ceiling. From above I could see myself standing and talking with Nosferatu hunched over by the window. It could all easily have been a dream. That occurred to me then; they say the brain during a dream is like a town at night, some functions do not work, and others are exceptionally active. My brain had been functioning in this way for months. Like in a nightmare.[21] A new one was beginning. And in it a person can say anything at all:

'I dreamt you. You came to my door. But I didn't understand what you wanted to tell me.'

I didn't perceive that this comment surprised him excessively. He was still staring through the window. However, he answered:

'I don't want to dream. And I have remembered many people.'

'Do you remember Aleksa?'

His head slowly turned towards me, I heard his bones creaking. Just when I thought I was going to see a scene from *The Exorcist*, the rest of his body turned too. Luckily...

'I have nothing to do with him. No sort of reckoning.'

He was pale, terribly thin, his skull was stretching his skin taut. In the reflection in his eyes I could see that I did not look much better.

'They told me to visit him and to tell him what he already knew. That was all I did.'

Of course, I asked him who told him that.

'The two of them. They had red hair. They said they would give me this flat if I did that. And I need the flat; from here I can keep track of that war criminal, Yankee.'

'What Yankee?'

'That one over there.' With his chin he pointed to the jail.

'That Yankee is in jail?'

He stared at the building. He did not blink. Maybe he had no eyelashes, for I did not notice then.

'Yes, but he has to come out some time. I shall wait however long it takes. He killed all my family. In front of my eyes.'

'Where is the little girl?' I turned to look around the room.

'What little girl?' He looked at me, and it seemed to me his eyes widened even more and became even more bloodshot.

'The one with a blonde ponytail...'

I thought I would drown in those eyes, that their sad, bloody darkness would suffocate me.

'She's gone. Because of her I must not and will not sleep.'

Our conversation lasted a lot longer than it takes to put it down on paper. He thought for a long time before answering, made big pauses in his sentences, stopped speaking as soon as someone appeared at the gates of the jail and then went on with the interrupted syllable. During one especially long pause I went to the window to see what had engrossed him so much.

The film director generously followed me. On the window there was only one little square cleaned, like a loop-hole for gunfire. I stood next to him and was aware of a strong smell, which I had never experienced before and which it is very hard for me to describe. It pressed the air out of my lungs, and the nausea spread from my stomach over my whole body. He turned around suddenly, I think I even heard the whistling of air; he grabbed me by the hand. His eyes were flashing.

'Look after yourself. The redheads have no heart. They are not of this world. They know what is under the earth.'

His nails were stabbing into my hand. I was afraid, of him, of his words... Yet I still asked, I had to...

'Please tell me, why have I been dreaming of you?'

He let go of my hand and looked earnestly into my face.

'You must not sleep! I was in the prison camp for six months and I didn't fall asleep even for one night. That's how I stayed alive,' he warned me, turning towards the window again. He tightened his thin lips and his eyes gazed towards some point outside. And I could, at last, again control my range of vision.

I shut the door quietly behind me. The lobby with no windows was a lot lighter than the room I had just left.

'Who is inside?' Mirna asked me.

I stood before her, breathing deeply and turning it all over deep in my mind. How could I tell her everything I wanted to; how could I convey to her at least a part of the things which had imprisoned my head in a red-hot crown. I sighed as profoundly as I could; I think I tried to explain like this, but I believe it was a lot more unintelligible. I spoke quickly, loudly and nervously:

'There is a man inside who has not slept for months. During the war his whole family was killed, and he ended up in the prison camp. Since then he has been trying to find the person who destroyed his life. He believes this man is in the jail. He doesn't seem like a spirit now, but like a man. He could easily be a spirit, because they exist. I'm sure of that, and your father believed in spirits too. I think the Pegasus brothers know where your father is. Aleksa thought they could lead him to you and your mother, and also to Perkman. Maybe because he knew the two of them were demons. True demons who can predict the end of the world.'

I said all that, took another breath and continued:

'My wife left me and I don't think she will ever come back. Her departure is my fault. I think only about that. I won't make the same mistake twice. Why shouldn't the two of us try? I can't stand solitude. And you are alone too, aren't you? Would you have searched for me otherwise?'

Leaning on the snowman, she looked at the snow. She was surprised, how could she not be, the last sentences had surprised me too. I wanted to lift up her head, to see what she was thinking;

if there was a reaction to my explanation, conclusion and overture. I think she turned and left in the middle of my sentence: 'It will be nice for us together; we'll read books, listen to music and talk about painting.'

I watched her leave, her footsteps becoming more rapid, becoming a race, then a solid sprint. She was running away as though from a lynch mob. It was one of the strongest blows to my vanity that I had ever suffered in my life.

I had made a mistake and I thought that alcohol might help me. Actually, I knew it would not help me, but I could not think of anything else.

The vodka was drinkable, fresh, sweet right from the first mouthful. I could not get enough. Quite predictably, the world slowly started to change. It became more interesting. I relaxed with a speed which made my ears burn. It was not important to me what anyone thought about me, they didn't even bother me. There were a lot of them, a real crowd, some bodies even touched me with their edges. They were sitting around me, calm, seemingly civilised, drinking, talking. The music was pleasant, it really was, I had no complaints, I remember very well, they were playing 'I Can't Take My Eyes Off of You'. I lit one cigarette after another, and enjoyed every puff. It was nice to be among people. Maybe soon I could even have started to smile. Stupidly and with glassy eyes, but smile just the same. The night was before me, amazing things could have happened.

But then Mirna came in. Angrily, she cut through the crowd with the help of her elbows, through the cries and curses, grabbed me by the hand, pulled me outside and pinned me in front of the window. She was shouting. A new play for the guests in the humble café bar. They had got a lot more than they could have expected for their money again. The waiter turned down the music so they could hear every word.

'I need money, understand? I have to pay back my loan in Sweden. All I wanted from you was that you use your journalist's influence and get rid of that madman from my apartment, so that I can sell it. Do you understand? I thought you had some contacts, that you know important people. Now I've found out you are not even a journalist any more...'

Two really ugly veins were pulsing on her forehead and neck. And her nose wrinkled in a not at all pretty way.

'I've lost too much time. The council could have solved my problems faster than you!'

Good, now things are quite clear, I thought. While she was taking breath for the next machine-gun burst, with which she probably hoped to finish me off, I said,

'If you've finished, I'd like to go back. I'm cold here.'

It seemed to me she wanted to say something else, but for me it was enough. I have a soul as well. I turned around and went inside. The people in the Sedmica café examined me for a moment, then the waiter turned up the sound of the music. Of course I remember (I already mentioned that this is one of my useless talents) that the song was 'Killing Me Softly'. Completely by chance. I ordered another vodka. I didn't feel bad. Really. Maybe, when you push a man roughly towards the bottom, that force makes him bounce up towards the surface and take another breath. Calmly I sat there, at ease with the unjust ways of the world; sipped my drink, enjoyed the music and watched through the glass the headlights of cars slipping through the night. One thing was finished, I thought optimistically; it's time to end the others as well.

Let's make use of this pause, and let's continue the humiliations. It's time for me to finally relate why my wife left me.

I can say straight away that everything that happened was my fault; but she started it. I know, we're not children, it's not important who started it, it's important how it finished, but that is the unadorned truth, there are no more reasons for lies. I remember, she was getting ready for the New Year celebrations. That was the first time we had celebrated New Year in town, in a restaurant. She wanted to order a new dress and asked me to help to find a model. I was not interested, I really wasn't. I don't understand anything about dresses, the meaning of the words pleated, flounced, embroidered, mignonette are completely unknown to me. She pushed a bundle of fashion magazines into my hands. She said, I well remember, 'I'll look just like you want me to!' Try to imagine what unbelievable possibilities are hidden inside that sentence! It's hard to imagine another with anything like the same strength. Who can reject such an offer? I was never a strong person – you have realised that by now, I believe – I have always been inclined towards all sorts of vices if it was possible to get to them easily and without consequences. My life, as Woody Allen says, revolved around cynicism, sarcasm, nihilism and orgasm.

She knew I liked to look at her, to measure her up as she passed through the room. When she asked me why I was watching her, I would roll my eyes and snort, in a caricature of animal passion. We were playing. Maybe she wanted to contribute to the game, to see how it would evolve. But I am certain she could not have known how it could finish. I didn't know either... I don't think anyone knows what they are hiding inside themselves, until the chance comes for it to awaken. I got my chance.

Vogue! What a word. When I say it, no matter how I practice the accent, I sound like an answering machine. That word and I do not belong to one another, I cannot use it in everyday conversation without feeling like an imposter. Written down, it turns into a symbol. And although until then I had never opened even one of the magazines, I read an infinite variety of information into that symbol; it covered me like a long block of advertisements: life without care, full of translucency, boats cutting through a calm sea, ivy-covered paths around houses, people sitting all day in constant sunlight in wicker chairs, wonderful women, proud, self-confident; there are bottles of wine lying in cellars, shoes like small idols, dresses that are precious pictures...That's simply how it is, I can't go against myself, these pictures assault me even though I read that *Vogue* is at fault for the death of hundreds of thousands of anorexic women, for severe, suicidal depression, broken marriages, infertility, curved spines, baldness. That it is as deadly as a nervous, dictatorial regime.[22] From the pile of magazines I took *Vogue*. Consciously. For the first time in my life...

I was blinded by Cartier jewels as radiant as an Amazonian snake. Already, on the next page, was the miracle of L'Oréal Panoramic Curl which enhances eyebrows and eyelashes so much that the lucky woman who owns it achieves the look of an Arab princess. I found out that something called Clinique exists – a new dramatically different gel; and another page brought a Tiffany brooch, magical like the arch of a mosque in Isfahan, which I had seen in a photograph. The 'In Vogue' column presented me with dramatic news from the latest fashion line, and a page called Style informed me that hysteria was ruling the world – the cause was a red dress in which every woman would become provocative. Another page in the same section was taken up with couples photographed while out strolling, and the captions said they were indeed beautiful, talented and together. I read a text about the evolution of the brassiere, the extraordinary wine produced by the Angove family, the fantastic ability of French women not to get fat; I saw how the photographer Mario Testino had given *Vogue* images of Elizabeth Hurley, Carolyn Murphy and Liya Kebede; I thought about the sentence: 'People who buy status symbols because they are status symbols are not doing it because they are materialistic or because they are greedy, they are simply sending a message: Please, be good to me.' *Vogue* recommended me a book, a CD, a film, told me 'what I needed to know' about new talents and gossip; and *Vogue Living* picked out glasses for me, plates and pillows (inspired by coral). While Bulgari jewellery, similar to forest flowers, intoxicated me, I learnt that Chanel Cristalle Gloss can at the same time make your lips sensual and natural and moreover give them a provocative shine, and that a Tag Heuer watch reveals what its owners are made of.

I turned the pages carefully, looking intently at the details, thinking about the way the editorial staff had planned the concept, looking for the method in creating titles and sub-titles, analysing the style of writing... No matter how hard I tried, I could not penetrate the secret of *Vogue*, find the source of the dark power, that rare essence which sets it apart from entire kiosks' worth of similar magazines. But when I closed the magazine I knew what I wanted. I wanted a *Vogue* woman – provocative, radiant, hard and ice-cold like platinum. I wanted a clone made out of the body parts of Chloë Sevigny, Cate Blanchett, Heidi Klum and Kirsten Dunst, directed by the cold mind of Anna Wintour.

I found such a woman in the 'Vogue Promotion' section, in an article called 'Summer Romance'. The editor had not written her name anywhere, for who knows what dark reasons, but for me she was the ideal woman, exactly the sort I had wanted to find. She was sitting in a black armchair. An armoured self-confidence emanated from her, she was aware she possessed the power of a multi-barrelled rocket launcher. She had bent one leg at her perfect knee, and stretched the other in front of herself, somewhere outside the shot, out of the magazine, in what was to me an unattainable continuation of a perfect world. She had placed one hand with long, pointed fingers on her hip, and with her other hand she embraced the back of the chair. She was not looking at the camera; her grey eyes were cynically fixed on my right shoulder, and her lips looked as though they were forming an aleph.[23] She wore a simple dress, of a colour somewhere between blue and green, without sleeves, with a small, sharp neckline. On the foot that I could see she wore a red sandal with three narrow straps. There was no jewellery. It was not necessary.

I was completely engrossed with the *Vogue* sprite, so that I did not notice when my wife came to stand behind me. I held the magazine out to her, open at the 'Summer Romance' page. Even though there were other photographs on it, she knew straight away which one had attracted me; she nodded her head and said,

'Right, we'll see what my dressmaker can do for you.'

Seven days passed. I returned home from the office and

immediately after a quick lunch lay down on the sofa. I was reading a book, having decided to quickly rid my mind of all the useless things I had had to repeat that day. I lifted my head when she called me. She was standing in front of me, her hair unrestrained, in that pretty *Vogue* dress and red sandals. She smiled, went to the chair and took up exactly the same pose as the model. I turned into a cannibal.

It was not making love, it was a devouring. Actually, the details of our pleasure are not important for the continuation of the story, why would a description of the numerous positions of love which we changed that day and a large part of the night be important to anyone else but us? The disclosure of the words we spoke to one another and similar details – how we were breathing, smiling, biting, shouting – would bring nothing to the understanding of the story.[24] It is enough to say that we loved one another better than ever. Our passion had the same strength as in the beginning of our relationship, but our confidence in the accuracy of our movements had grown much stronger.

Her transformation had a very powerful effect on me. It seemed to me that a completely new tunnel had opened up in life, full of exciting and unknown channels. The hope was born in me that I had found the way, with no risk or effort at all, to possess all women in the world. Simply, I would change my wife, the body I already possessed I would adapt to resemble the one I wanted.

As soon as I noticed the small signs of a lessening of passion, I found a new dress, black with red flowers. When she drew her fingers into the silk gloves, she turned into a mistress of the senses. You will have to believe what I say... After that the hunger became greater, but clothes could no longer satisfy me. I wanted a complete transformation. I asked her to tie her hair in a tight bun and to wear a minimum of make-up. I wanted her to wear a white blouse and black skirt, which wrapped her body tightly and reached two fingers above her knees. I wanted the attitude that went with those clothes – severe and arrogant. I wanted to hear the high heels of her shoes ringing out decisively on the parquet, to see how in amazement, or disdain, she lifted up one eyebrow, fully aware of her perfect figure. I wanted the Snow Queen, a manageress made of steel, a bureaucratic goddess. (I wanted, you must excuse me, to have Anna Wintour, in case you haven't already realised that.) And I wanted her to always be like that, not just in the bedroom. I pleaded with her to find such a being inside herself. We made love on the writing table and I demanded she spoke rude words; that she continually described what was happening to her. (It's important that I emphasize the details here.) She consented, but I remember now, she unfailingly added:

'I will, if it means so much to you.'

When that too bored me, I wanted her to look like Patti Smith. I chose a singlet, helped to alter the jacket, found a brooch in the form of a horse; she dyed her hair black by herself and cut an uneven fringe. I asked her to squat down and hold onto the radiator, completely naked. She also looked wonderful as Holly Golightly too, in a white dress and with a hat on her head. We listened to 'Moon River' a lot in those days. I can't stand that song now.

One evening, I remember, the football fans were celebrating a win under our window. They were tooting car horns, singing 'how great it is to see you again'; it was impossible to think from all the noise. She sat on my favourite chair by the window, dressed only in a wide blue singlet (like Betty Blue). She had an unusual expression on her face, some sort of complete absence of mind, but with such sadness. I thought it was a part of her act, and then I heard a deep, deep sigh and the words,

'Why can't you love me the way I am?'

Such a question got me up from the armchair in front of the television. We had never had such a dramatic conversation before. I sat down opposite her and saw tears in her eyes.

'But, I do love you, I truly love you.' I think I murmured that or something very like it.

'I asked you why you can't love me, just me, and not this daydream?' she raised her tone of voice.

I repeated my last sentence.

Now she was already shouting, 'Why can't I be myself?'

'You can, really you can.' Finally I realised the games were over.

'But, I can't!' she screamed.

'You can, why can't you? You can right now. Be whatever you like. Be my guest.'

'I can't.' She was crying now.

'Why not?'

'Because, you idiot, I can't remember what I was like!'

From this whole sentence, one word upset me the most. Idiot. It was the first time I had heard her say it. She had called me names before, let's not lie about this, different insulting expressions like fool, catfish, horse, beast, cretin, but never, ever had she used the word 'idiot'. The word 'idiot' was not our word. It was the word of a strange woman, cold and sharp, a television word, legal, bureaucratic, a nothing word. The rest of the sentence was not without interest either, but that word, I felt, was the most important. 'Idiot', without a doubt, definitely divided us.

When I came home from work the next day, she was not in the apartment. And she never came back.

And that was that.

Since then I have been alone. I know what loneliness is, I know how a man can easily become transparent. To lessen the fear of being invisible I often used to count my own qualities, as a sort of psychotherapy – I'm still young, the grey hairs on my temple denote manliness and not old age; I am not excessively attractive, but I don't believe that if someone were describing me they would first say I was ugly; I can be interesting in company, if I avoid alcohol I can even be charming; I am compassionate. I often reminded myself of exploits of seduction, even those for which I was not quite certain whether they had happened as I recollected them; evoked all the compliments women had ever sent my way, remembered their faces...

In this way I got as far as Mirna. She was the only woman who had walked directly into my life. Is it so strange that I thought

I could try? Was my offer so shocking? I was sure she was not indifferent towards me. Because, why had she chosen to knock on my door, to seek me out for help and not someone else? I am not an influential person, that's clear, neither am I known for my strength, pushiness or wisdom. There are countless more suitable people than I who could, with no fuss at all and in a short time, find her father. We shouldn't ignore the body language either, I had read about it in a magazine; how she leant against me, how she gazed at me, smiled...

It's obvious you shouldn't believe what the magazines tell you; but when I thought about it as I sat in the bar, I concluded it didn't matter; at least one more dilemma had been resolved. To give myself courage, I drank to the health of the loudspeaker and whispered into my glass,

'If this evening is the solution, then let it never end. Hey Lou, this is the beginning of a beautiful adventure.'

A lemon slice rotated in the liquid.

Three vodkas after that I decided that I would visit the Pegases and talk to them. Two more vodkas, three songs alongside them, and I was looking for a taxi out on the street.

And, of course, I found Ekrem.

In Ekrem's taxi it smelt of pineapple. Cardboard trees were swaying on the rear-view mirror, and on the radio, through the crackling of the vinyl, some woman was singing a folk song. The sky was luminous, with little bits of confetti thrown around. We left the town, with the yellow windows of houses skipping past the car. Then the moon took over the lighting, and everything became silver. We had travelled less than ten minutes, and already we had arrived in uninhabited country, large fields under snow, old pathways leading into black forest to places and things I didn't dare think about. The land around us was completely empty; the snow left untouched. A huge empty living space. And we had fought and died so sweetly for every little bit of land, for small dry hills, for impenetrable thickets, muddy glades, dead pear trees, gravel pits, water-worn gullies. The taxi stopped in front of big steel gates.

Ekrem turned towards me.

'I don't want to go any further. Don't you go either. Surely, neighbour, I can talk you out of it?' he asked me.

I shook my head and got out.

'As you wish. I'll wait for you,' I heard behind me.

I pushed the gate and stepped onto the yellow brick path. It went through a corridor of winged plaster horses, towards a strong light on the top of a small hill. After about a hundred metres and two troops of horses, I saw the Pegasus Motel. It looked like an ice-cream sundae. Under dozens of bright floodlights it shone in all imaginable colours, studded with cupolas, randomly pierced with round windows, balconies and verandas... In front of it, on tall poles, flags of all the countries of the European Union were hanging, and under them were parked expensive, shiny cars. Like in Brussels, or some other town where important people live. In front of the door of the motel stood a doorman dressed in the uniform of the Yugoslav navy. He did not even look at me, he just smartly opened the door. Two huge guards were standing in front of a woven basket full of pistols, knives, sprays, sticks, stakes, knuckle-dusters, chains... They informed me I could not go in with weapons and looked disappointed when I told them I was unarmed.

Inside it was hot, suffocating, humid and smelly. Like the inside of a meat pie. Loud bass from the ceiling nailed us to the floor, keyboards were spluttering from all corners, accordions shrieking, clarinet pipes discharging, all the trumpets of the world coming into the folk-song refrain where the word 'uzurlikzurli' waited for a Diva to strip off her fur coat, loosen her hair, throw away her panties, brassiere, respectability and call for us to kill ourselves with merriment. It was a grandiose 'folkateque', full of attractive girls dressed like porn stars. They were dancing in front of mirrors and moving their hips between the laser beams. The few men on the dance floor did not know how to dance; most of them simply throwing out their arms and falling on their knees in front of the beauties, kissing their stomachs, squeezing their buttocks, biting their crotches, licking their piercings, gnashing their teeth, panting and howling.

The biggest number of males were jostling each other around the bar and watched the dancing. I noticed that they weren't talking to one another, so happily joined them.

'Double vodka, with lots of lemon,' I asked a thin waiter in a pink singlet.

Briefly, but with withering cynicism, he measured me up and down and then turned to the shelves with the glasses. From there he sent word back to me, 'We don't serve guests who are already drunk.'

His reaction was totally unexpected; especially since I was in a den where not one person was in his right mind. I told him this, but it didn't seem fluster him in the least.

'True. But, they all got nicely drunk here with us. And you have come from who knows where and who knows whose pockets you have filled until now. You planned to drink one drink here, look at the birds, make some sort of trouble and then throw up in our WC. And then I would have to clean it up. Well, you fuckin' won't!'

I was once a respected person in town, not so long ago. Restaurant owners were happy when they saw me, waiters were deferential...

'Where are your bosses?' I asked him seriously.

'Maybe you have a complaint?'

'I have to see them, I came here because of them.'

'The bosses are in the VIP room.'

'Tell them I'm a journalist.'

'Really? From *Express*?'

I could see he was beginning to like me, so I lied.

'Yes, that's right.'

'We like you people from *Express*. Next week Seka Aleksić is going to sing here. Feel free to write that.'

'I will; and the bosses?'

He thought for a little while and then decided.

'They read *Express* too... Let's go to the VIP room.'

We went from behind the bar into a narrow corridor. The walls were covered with the stuffed heads of animals. The horns were crossed at the ceiling and made a thorny vault.

The room into which we went reminded me of a jewellery box. It was perfectly round and from floor to ceiling lined with red velour. In the centre of the room was planted a golden pole, and enclosing this was a red plush sofa. A naked girl was dancing around the pole, even though I heard no music; even the bass from the discothèque could not reach us here. A huge red-haired man was sitting on the sofa, dressed in a dark business suit with a tie, surrounded by four girls who of all the different clothes they could have been wearing had on only red shoes with high metal heels. The man was saying something to them, and they were listening to him carefully. Like a moment in nature. Behind them, another man, much thinner but with much more luxurious red hair, like cotton candy, sat in front of a huge computer screen playing a game – one of those games where the player has the role of an omnipotent being who creates and destroys worlds.

The waiter went up to the large man, briefly whispered in his ear and left. No-one from this unusual company paid any attention to me. The dancer was smiling at the ceiling. I approached the sofa, coughed and asked, 'Are you...'

The giant did not turn around, he just said, 'Please address me correctly, we do not know each other.'

'Sorry, sir, but are you...'

He interrupted me again, but this time he looked at me with shining eyes.

'Excuse me, sir, I just need to finish my train of thought,' and he turned back to the girls.

He expounded this 'thought' to them, I remember it well:

'You don't consider things, and men don't like stupid women. For instance, you don't know how to listen to poetry. The most important things for you are to get drunk and to dance. You must know, music is an art; in song you have to look for meaning hidden to ordinary people. And we are not ordinary people, or ordinary women. Isn't that so? I'll take as an example the song 'Mejra in Her Coffin'. You think you know it well. You've heard it a million times, but you don't know what it is really all about... Isn't that so? That's why I am here and I'll tell you what the problem is. We'll start with the first verse which says, *The water is coming from hill to hill.* The song-writer wants to say that a flood has burst out and that the water has filled the valley. He continues, *It carries Mejra in her coffin.* This means the flood has caused a landslide and thrown Mejra, who was probably buried not long ago, out of her grave. Then the song says, if I am not mistaken: *Come with us, Mejra, have dinner with us,* That means the water carried the girl through the village or settlement, we can't know; that her friends and maybe her relatives saw her – the poet does not tell us this precisely either – and that they asked her to come to dinner. Continuing, the poet says, in a fantastic way, because how can a dead person speak, but that is poetic licence, *Have dinner, don't wait for me, dinner is waiting for me in Paradise with the Houris.* So, Mejra is informing them that they cannot be her company, because they are alive, and she is dead, and that because of that she would prefer to eat something in Paradise with the Houris. In this verse we also find out that Mejra, during her life, was a true believer and so can count on a place in Paradise, or Heaven, whichever is to your liking, depending on your religion. Is it clear to you now?'

The girls did not answer, so he turned towards me.

'Am I not right, journalist?'

The gaze from his little eyes danced across my face like a sniper's target.

'He's not a journalist, it's a long time since he was a journalist. Now he is a depressive idler.' The man in front of the computer had a squeaky voice, as though it were broadcast from a tiny radio.

The giant pursed his lips. It seemed to me that his big teeth were moving behind them.

'Stay a little longer with us,' he said to me and then turned again to the girls. He continued his lecture.

The giant said: 'You have to educate yourselves, and the easiest and quickest way to do that is by watching television. You have televisions in your rooms, and digital aerials which can get as many as 800 channels for you. But you have to carefully choose content which will be useful.'

The thin one continued to play his game: he sent a group of workers into the forest to cut the wood necessary for building houses and farms.

I imagined morning coffee in a nice little café beneath the trees. A spring morning, leaves of a delicate whispering green, newspapers rustling, some woman's hands opening the window of the house over the road.

The giant: 'You have to follow all the news programs. If an exceptionally important client comes in, someone who demands special treatment, you don't have to watch the entire late-night news right to the end, but you must unfailingly watch the headlines. I'm the only one who stipulates who those important clients are.'

The thin man: He built a barracks for the soldiers and turned a few peasants into archers and spearmen. He increased their rations of meat and cheese.

Me: I remembered fish dinners on the island of Hvar, boats lit up with white Chinese lanterns, pastry-cooks juggling scoops of ice-cream, water roaring in my ears.

The giant: 'I recommend all the programs about nature and animals. You can learn more about people from them than about animals. Circle popular science programs in the television guide, especially the ones about space, black holes, stars, the Milky Way, comets – he who doesn't know how things are in space, doesn't know about the earth either. Watch programs about culture too, you have to know what is being written about, but it isn't necessary to know how and why; remember the names of painters, see what is the modern way of showing the world today.'

The thin man: He formed two troops of soldiers, strengthened the walls of the trap, littered pitch on the approaches. He put up huts for the woodcutters. Made extra storerooms for the weapons.

Me: It's afternoon. Summer. The window shutters are down. It's quiet and the whole town is resting. I am lying in bed with my wife and caressing her breasts. She has shut her eyes.

The giant: 'Soap operas should also be considered regular viewing. They will help you to exercise your emotions. You are as cold as ice, and the clients don't like that. In just one episode of a soap opera you have the complete scale of emotions: happiness, passion, desire, ecstasy, maybe a little jealousy, sadness, anger, but just a little bit... No need to overdo it, fuck your ancestors.'

The thin man: 'Don't swear!'

Unnaturally quickly for such a large man, the giant turned towards me.

'Have I spoken truly, sir? If you are not a journalist, you certainly watch television. I don't know even one man who does not have a television in his home.'

The thin player puts the spearmen around the king's castle and makes the remark:

'He has a television, but he hardly ever watches it. He is not a journalist, but he poses questions.'

'And so what?' The giant was looking at me, yet asking his brother.

'I know what, but I would like him to tell us.'

'He can, he will relate it all to us. Without fail. As soon as I finish this meeting with the girls. He will wait.'

Once he uttered this, his eyes turned completely white, I was sure. He turned again to the naked students.

The giant: 'I noticed that the hygiene in your rooms is not to a satisfactory standard. You must fix that at once. I abhor rubbish, surely you won't make a rubbish tip out of our motel?'

The thin man: The enemy was coming closer to the trap. They had sent a unit to attack. With catapults and spears they showered the enemy army, and the infantry burnt everything before them.

Me: I could not get rid of the picture of crunching teeth squeezing a walnut.

The giant: 'Have you ever been to the rubbish tip?'

All at once I realised the girls had left the room. The question was directed towards me.

The giant: 'Imagine how much rubbish a man leaves behind him before he dies. We can estimate the daily amount, let's say yours. I'm sure you smoke at least twenty cigarettes a day – so, cigarette butts and ash, packets, newspapers, milk cartons, plastic bags, boxes, cellophane, food remnants, peelings, stubs, some tins...'

The thin man: He aimed the spearmen at the little hill, bombarded the enemy cavalry, and immediately after the word 'tins' he joined in:

'He doesn't eat tinned food or milk. He only eats biscuits, and the only dietary supplement is Ultra ABC Plus vitamin tablets.' (I really do use these tablets, at least until I get my organism used to a meagre diet.)

Me: I thought nothing. I tried to withstand the gaze from the white eyes.

The giant: 'Okay, but faeces are there too, all sorts of discharges that his body lets loose from time to time, I don't have to list them... He needs clothes, shoes, fuel. All of those needs pollute or mutilate nature. Besides that, the man doesn't spare nature, he's extravagant and leaves a lot of waste that could be used.'

The thin man: 'Yes, truly our dear guest leaves a lot of rubbish behind. He is asking about Aleksandar Ranković, he's been to the Music School...' (He looked at me, beaming, in raptures because I was standing before him. I was like a toy for which he had waited a long time. There was something carnivorous in his gaze).

Me: Into my mind came the sight of an old fig tree, even though I do not know exactly what a fig tree looks like. Under the fig tree was a pile of stones with numerous dark openings from which were inching the tails and heads of red snakes.

The giant: 'Except for a small amount of faeces, animals leave nothing behind them. In nature they behave in exactly the right way, like a good host. They even hide their bodies carefully. Has anyone ever seen any graveyards of animals, pigeons, deer or cats?'

The thin man: 'His wife left him and since then he has suffered greatly because of that. For a whole nine months and three days he was masturbating in bed. During that time his wife went over the limit. How old is she, thirty-five if I am not mistaken? Interesting, I think she is more beautiful than ever, her breasts are fuller, and she has covered those ugly bones on her hips with meat.'

Me: The room had become a digestive tract, the walls were pulsating.

The giant: 'Our towns are surrounded by cemeteries. The oldest cemetery in France is no older than the end of the eighteenth century. Until then, when a cemetery became full, in order to make room for new corpses, the poor people's bones were dug up and used to fill up walls in castles. They believed human bones made good insulation.'

The thin man: 'Tell him you can't sleep' (squeaky voice).

Then I realised I could go no further. Or more exactly, go no lower. I should have been grateful to the red-haired rat for giving me such a clear picture. I should have been grateful to him for the final realisation that I can control absolutely nothing. Neither around me, nor inside me. Whatever I do, I can't change anything. Fear, wailing, running away, hiding – none of them have any sense any more. I have nothing to protect, nothing to be afraid of, no reason to evade people and wrap myself away from them. And my co-inhabitant seemed to have come to the same conclusion, for he straightened his body, grew tall, roared and filled me with hissing fury. Like my neighbour's pigeons, the two of us went into attack formation, rose on our hind legs, pulled tight all our bones, muscles, nerves. Our joints snapped, veins squeaked, blood gushed. Everything around us was red, shining, neon-lit. We jumped into the redness, without any plan or goal, just full of the desire to pulverise everything in front of us.

It seems to me we were flying, for at least five seconds, I think I succeeded in swinging my fists a few times... And then I hit something hard, something quite impenetrable. A terrible pain cramped me, suddenly redness gushed into my head, a million tons of crimson colour exploded in geysers, a billion little eruptions... After the last drop of red had gushed, everything became black.

All things are actually black in their own nature; they change only when you expose them to light. Because of this, Leonardo began every one of his paintings with a layer of black colour. I was lying plunged into black colour. From the blackness one piece broke off, trembled, swayed and turned into the Man with the Bloodshot Eyes. He bent over me and said,

'You're sleeping, and you told me you couldn't.'

'Help me to get up,' I asked him.

'I can't, I have to go. I won't stay here any longer,' he said and went into a whirlpool of darkness which closed behind him.

Blackness embraced me again. I don't know how long I was lying in it before I heard a soft song and the deep voice of the giant who was reciting above it.

Who stole from the night the blackest colour and pressed it
    into your eyes and gave them lustre, Romana?
Who forces the birds to give up their voices, to become dumb
    and lose their breath before you, Romana?
What is the fire of a volcano, compared to the volcano of
    ardour whose blaze you throw at us in your dance, Romana?
And all eyes want to yearningly pursue you and all hands
    wish at least to touch you, Romana.
One night for you, I was your song, a song already forgotten
    tomorrow, Romana.
Because your restless love which belongs to a world apart
    from me is stronger than passion, Romana.
Better I never saw you or wanted you, better I pay with my
    life, if I were to lose you.

'Songs like this are not sung any more, there is no longer any real art. In it all is as it should be, unrequited love truly and rightfully described. Isn't that so, journalist, or whatever you are?'

'He doesn't work as a journalist, but people still think that is his job,' I heard the squeaky voice explain.

I decided to come out of the dark; I clenched my teeth, pulled my head into my shoulders and tried to push through the membrane, to stand up. The membrane became tighter, it squeezed my head, pain filled my eyes... I did not succeed. I heard loathsome whistling.

'A man is made up of his terrors. The more terrors you have, the more man you are. Unless I am mistaken, you only have seven. And I, without meaning to boast, I have none at all. That says a lot about me.'

I had to get rid of the voices. I gathered all my strength, closed my eyes, clenched my teeth, turned every little part of my body into a spring. And I succeeded. The membrane broke with a strong explosion. And everything around me was white.

'Do you want some Caffetin?' The same squeaky voice was waiting for me. 'Only that can help you, isn't that right?'

* * *

I awoke in clean whiteness. I have always imagined a nun's room would look like that – clean, narrow bed, white bedside cupboard, small hand basin, a narrow table with two white chairs. Now when I think about it, it must have been one of the rooms in which the girls received clients in the motel. I was lying in the lap of one of them. She was very attractive, although, if I were to be a bit fussy, I did not really like her hairdo. She was holding a cold towel to my head, and her large-nippled, naked breasts dangled over my head. The Pegases were sitting on the small chairs. Both of them had interlaced their fingers and had one eyebrow held up in a mark of attention, like a board of examiners. The thin one smiled sparsely and said,

'He is Albin; I am Aldin, older than he by eight minutes.[25] We are brothers, we have the same surname – Pegasus. Like the winged horse. My name means "the sublimity of faith", and his does not mean anything. Your name means "smiling", but it is not appropriate for you, because you have not truly smiled for at least ten years. You could certainly find some meaning in that, but it is not the theme of our conversation.'

Aldin raised his hand and the girl went out, conspicuously wiggling her naked bottom.

'You survived a collision with Albin. That's an unpleasant experience even for people much stronger than you. But, don't worry, you only have a headache, it could have been a lot worse. We are at your disposal and will answer all your questions. What interests you?'

I could not of course have supposed that this would be so easy. I never dreamt the Pegases would ever concern themselves with me, want to converse with me, even let me ask questions. Even though I was completely surprised, I said, unceremoniously, 'Aleksa,' and the sound of every letter, it seemed to me, made a scar on my brain. Even though I am a veteran of migraines, I had never met a headache like that before.

'Aleksa. So that's the first question. All right. We know him. Aleksandar Ranković is a good man. Our mother loved his programs. She was always listening to them. I remember, once she said that Aleksa was the only person in the whole town who spoke with her. I did not understand that then, but now it is quite clear to me. I don't want to talk about that any more. It is enough to say that, in remembrance of our mother, we helped him during the war.'

I continued with my interrogation.

'So, where is Aleksa? The last trace of him says that he was to meet with you...'

Albin widened his eyes. Aldin calmly replied, 'You read that in his diary, didn't you?'

'How do you know?'

'I know, I know everything, get used to it... With time I have forgotten about Aleksa. You see, only now do I realise I haven't seen him for years. War is an interesting time, lots of things happen and it's hard to concentrate on one thing.'

'So?' I think that is how I asked, bravely.

They paid no attention to my mustering of courage.

'He wanted us to take him to the open cut.'

Aldin suddenly interrupted the sentence. The brothers looked at one another, briefly. Albin spoke,

'Rest a while, we'll take you home. Your dear neighbour Ekrem will take you. '

I didn't want to go. I wanted answers. I don't know what answers I expected, but I thought everything would be better if I asked, if I knew and understood.

'Why did you send that poor prison camp inmate to Aleksa's door?'

Again they looked at one another. Aldin nodded, Albin answered,

'Even though during the war more people died than in normal times, there were not enough vacant apartments. Probably because houses were burned, I don't believe it was because of procreation.'

Aldin continued, 'The man needed a place to stay, and Aleksa was spurred to go. I told you, we are the inspiration.'

They smiled at one another. I continued with my questions. I am not brave, and I am not trying to hide that. But, sometimes in life there comes a time when a man breaks faith with his nature.

'Did you torture Aleksa in the Music School?'

'You're full of questions, but don't be nervous, we'll tell you everything. The Music School is indeed an interesting topic.'

Aldin was now quite serious, his annoying smile was gone.

'That's where we met Aleksa. He tried to get in but the guard wouldn't let him. He was shouting that he wanted to see what was happening, that he wanted to find out for himself. I went out and told him that his life would not change in the least, neither could he change the lives of others, no matter what he saw.'

Albin added, 'He asked us if we were killing people inside.'

Aldin continued, 'We told him the two of us had not even killed one person. Just as we told you, too.'

Albin again added, 'Except that he was satisfied with the answer.'

'But you are not; you are fascinated by death. Fuck death. Like it's some particularly special thing. People die every day and they die easily. It's unbelievable how easily, that's interesting. They disappear so quickly and with them everything that was only theirs, that they thought was special, different, things because of which they valued themselves, things they were ashamed of. They take everything with them. A huge part of the world. And the world makes a new arrangement and everything is again back to the beginning.'

I had more questions, I had a thousand questions... 'Why did you do that, I can't understand? Why did you torture people? What did you want from them?'

'Can't you imagine? You really don't know?'

I don't know which of the two asked me, maybe both of them, but I remember the answer. I remember the answer perfectly.

'The Music School is our gift to the town. After all the awful things that have happened there, the town is no longer innocent and won't be ever again. Whenever a lot of people are together in the same place and they start to talk to one another about how lovely the town is, how civilised, how gentle, and the people in it good people, someone is going to remember the Music School.'

'That's stupid. And pathetic, ' I said. 'I can't believe everything you did was because of that.'

They looked at one another.

'Okay, maybe it wasn't only that. There was money; gold, beautiful women and fast horses.'

They laughed. Gruesomely, of course. All at once, Aldin jumped up from the chair and was right in my face. Eau de Cologne, a little sweat, hair lacquer and anger. He shouted,

'What do you think, do you think you are innocent? You knew

about the Music School, you must have heard what was happening! You're also guilty if you didn't hear, guilty because you weren't worried about other people, you were thinking only about your own head. You're guilty too!'

His anger was growing. He threw his arms apart as though he wanted to move the walls.

'Everyone is guilty, no-one is innocent. Everyone is looking for the easiest way to get to nice things. They don't care at all that the people who fulfil their desires work like slaves, die of strange illnesses, that chemicals eat them up, polluted air suffocates them. They knowingly pay so that others kill for them, torture, humiliate people. No-one is innocent, no-one. Fuck all your mothers! Those who hear and those who don't!'

And then he calmed down. Suddenly.

'You know what, maybe it wouldn't be bad if you asked Ahmed where Aleksa is. You know, he called us to help him.'

He saw that I was surprised. That made him happy.

'Well, well, you didn't know. I'm telling you, no-one is innocent, no-one. And now pull yourself together. Ekrem is waiting, our old comrade-in-arms from the Music School.'

He delighted in the expression on my face.

'You didn't know that either? What sort of journalist are you? You're a dickhead of a journalist. Go on now, so he doesn't have to wait. He has a soul too, even if he is a taxi driver.'

Ekrem was silent in the car. I was holding my head in my hands, trying to think.

'I told you you didn't need this,' he said, finally.

'And did you need the Music School?'

I was looking at him, directly into his eyes. It wasn't easy, because his gaze was quivering in the depths, ready to hide. But I succeeded, I caught him and held him tightly. The smile left his face.

'Get out of the car!'

I got out.

I had only been able to take a step when he opened the door. He could hardly calm his anger while he said through his teeth, 'I live from driving people wherever they want to go, from this world to the next, if needs be and if they can pay. I don't choose who gets into my car, neither am I interested in why someone goes wherever. Is that clear? If it's clear then get in the car and tell me where you want me to drive you.'

I got in. It would have been stupid not to agree. I was in the middle of the forest, in the middle of the night. It was cold and obviously I had used up a few decades' worth of obstinacy.

Crushed by fatigue, I slowly unlocked the door of the flat. I was ready for the worst. When a person has met the Pegases there are very few things left which can surprise him. I would not have been surprised even if the door of the flat had lead into the most terrible apparitions of fantastic zoology – into the three throats of the monster Aheron and in them tears, gnashing of teeth, unbearable scorching heat, biting cold, dogs, bears, lions and rattlesnakes.[26] But the door opened unpretentiously into my bachelor flat. Stale air. I turned on the light in the corridor and... Nothing. The usual thing. I stepped onto the parquet and it groaned. As always. I sat on the chair next to the window and listened, though I am not sure what I really wanted to hear. It was pleasant. I thought my restless subtenant had at last left me. That I was quite alone. Alone in my own skin, comfortably tucked into my cosy skeleton. I planned to sleep for a month, but in a healthy way, like an industrious worker. Before that I would take care of a few more important jobs. The first was to visit Ahmed, and then to inform the police. To denounce the Pegases and put an end to their stupid revenge. I did not even want to think about what sort of evil could satisfy them and finally calm them.

On the wall of the bedroom I found a long crack. It looked like the varicose vein on an old hairdresser's leg. I wondered what could have caused it to appear. Perhaps the town had suffered an earthquake, and I had slept through it. It was a bad crack; but a good plasterer could easily get rid of it.

The telephone was ringing frantically.

'Are you okay?'

Even though the previous days had been full of surprises, I had not expected this call. I stopped breathing, my mouth was dry, and my brain was revolving numerous combinations of possible answers at the same time, completely undecided as to which one to choose. It was the voice of my ex-wife. Full of love and anxiety! Like it had used to be. I think I could have achieved an orgasm from it.

'Yes, I am,' I whispered excitedly, panting like a dog on a hot day.

'A friend of yours called me. He said you were in terrible trouble and that you needed help.'

'Which friend?'

'I asked him that too. He laughed and said: *from the Music School*. He laughed in a horrible way. Like a madman... Who is that man?'

Nothing was pleasant any more. The Pegases had telephoned her. They had known that I truly cared about only one person in the world. My wife (I know, my ex-wife...)

'Don't be afraid, Romana. Everything will be all right,' I said. She was silent.

'Truly, this time everything will be all right.'

'We'll see...'she said very, very quietly, and put down the receiver.

I went back to the chair. I felt like an extra heart was beating in my chest.

I couldn't allow anything to happen to her. Everything that used to be good rested in her. I couldn't imagine her face next to the Pegases. As if they are living in parallel worlds, made up of different materials, which nothing can bring together. Beings of light and darkness must always be separate, otherwise the balance of the world would be disrupted and everything that was worth anything at all would be fucked.

I had to give up, forget about the police, justice, revenge. I couldn't bring her into this dirty story. I was horrified even at the thought that she had spoken to them. I could not allow the horrible brothers to come into her life. I could not do that to her. Not for anything in the world.

Before going to sleep I enjoyed remembering that short sentence of Romana's: 'Are you okay?' I thought about what wonderful things could be found in it. It seemed clear from those three words that she still cared about me, because why else would she be worried? She had not whispered, she had spoken fairly loudly, so where then was her new man while she was talking to me? Maybe she had not called from home or maybe he had not been in the flat? For pleasant dreams I chose the third, most agreeable variable – he was there, but she phoned regardless of him, she didn't care what he thought. She had realised that I was the most important thing in her life. Phenomenal.

* * *

Mustafa's voice woke me. Quite clearly I heard the morning message, 'Better that I pay with my life, if I lose you'. All the skin on my body tightened. Immediately came the thought that something must have happened to Romana. Even though the verse could be interpreted in more than one way, I chose the worst. I had to do everything I could to protect her. At first, a terrible nervousness overcame me, I could have slid out of my skin, like soap from a fist. I rushed out of the apartment building and began to run through the streets. Then I realised I did not know where she now lived. After this realisation, I still ran for another fifteen minutes, I don't know why, perhaps hoping I would somehow come across her. In the end, completely wet and without even one decent molecule of oxygen in my lungs,

I stopped. I stood there up to my knees in snow and tried to think. I remembered I had not seen her since she came for her things. Maybe she had left town; surely she had, for she never liked it, I thought. And then I again played over in my mind the short track of our last conversation and stopped at the very end. It was quiet, maybe I had not heard properly; maybe she said 'Be seeing you' and not 'We'll see'.

I'm like that. I'm able to interpret everything to my liking, even when everything points quite clearly to the fact that I am mistaken. This talent is justifiably called 'hysterical blindness'.

* * *

I found Ahmed in his office. He was not happy when he saw me. He was sitting gloomily at the table. There was no chessboard in front of him, and on the wall above his head was just a clear rectangle. He could see that I was looking at the place where the blind horse had been.

'If you've come to talk about ghosts, that stupidity doesn't interest me.'

I sat down, put my elbows on the table, looked him directly in the eyes (he turned his gaze away) and said, 'I've come to talk about Aleksa...'

'I said I don't want to talk about ghosts!'

He got up, took his coat and went out. I knew he wanted me to follow him.

The waiter brought our drinks without asking anything. That nice herbal brandy. It smelt like the whole Mediterranean. I poured it down my throat. It didn't deserve to be treated like that.

Ahmed did not touch his glass. He was rinsing his mouth with a sip of water. When he had finally swallowed it he said, 'If you really want me to, I can tell you how I used to morbidly envy Aleksa.'

I let him know I agreed by asking the waiter for another brandy. His confession, like everything until now, I have reconstructed from memory. I think I have remembered very well; he spoke evenly, without pausing, stuttering or repeating himself, as though he had been preparing the speech for a long time. This is what he said:

'Yes, I envied him. I envied him for having Anđela and Mirna. Because they loved him as they did. While I was sitting in their flat and while they tried to make me feel like a member of the family, my stomach was prickling with envy. Because of that I stopped going to see them. We met mostly in my office; in the library it was not so obvious how much happier he was than I. I was terribly ashamed of my jealousy; I was happy when over time I felt it was slowly giving way. When they left, I was annoyed by his continual wailing about how he was now alone, how he missed his wife and daughter, how he thought he was going slightly mad. How could he have been so blind, how could he have been so cruel? He knew I had been alone all my life, he knew I had no-one that I could have missed... And still, he continued, every day... Every God-given day he came to my office and snivelled. It was harder for me than the war.'

He spoke softly, almost whispered. He was breathing heavily, his ears were red and I even thought he might become ill.

'Everything became even worse when he told me he had seen Perkman... Just like that... He saw him without any effort at all, without research, without the indispensable dedication. The spirit actually found *him*. My envy returned once more, worse than ever; I couldn't look him in the eyes because of it. I had devoted my whole life to searching for spirits, and never saw even one. I gave up everything for that, nothing else interested me. I don't know modern literature, film, sport, theatre, painting, except if it has something to connect it to my obsession. I don't watch television, I don't understand what is modern or what the difference is between political parties. Most of the time I'm alone. Who can put up with such a man for long? Yet that didn't bother me, not while I believed I still had a lot of time ahead. But, the time comes when a man starts to count the years and works out that he has forgotten more years than are left to him.

It was only then that I was crushed by the knowledge that I would spend that wretched remainder alone. The worst thing is that I know I have wasted the years. I squandered everything in a search for something I have never seen, something in which I have no reason to believe. And Aleksa... That one got everything without any effort at all. I called the Pegases because of that, I told them to take him somewhere, to hell and back if they wanted to, as long as it was far away from me.'

I got up from the chair; the waiter came up to me, helped me into my coat and saw me to the door. I got out my wallet, and the waiter waved his hand.

'No need, my shout. This evening is the last night, we're shutting the bar for good.' He inclined his head and danced away.

He went up to Ahmed's table and turned off the light. Darkness swallowed up the old man.

* * *

I really don't know any more if it was night, day, morning. The crack above the bed in the bedroom was clearly visible. It had become wider, so that now a pencil could have passed through it. I tried... I put my hand over it and felt a slight movement of air. Impossible, it was not an outer wall.

I shut the door, sat on my chair and decided not to think any more about that or about anything else. To just sit there, like in that joke. I succeeded quite well in keeping a big black blotch in my head. Darkness.

Right up until I heard someone knock very lightly on the wood of the door, maybe with the nail of an index finger. I was in such a state that I could have heard ants' legs scraping in their narrow tunnels under the parquet.

Mirna was standing in the doorway. She had an unusual expression on her face; a mixture of sadness and kind-heartedness. Obviously, I simply can't describe it, and it seems as if there are more and more such discrepancies in this story. I did not let her come into the apartment. The walls were groaning. It would have been quite impolite to take a guest into such distress. I shut the door behind me. We stood on the stairs, in the silence of the dead apartment building. She took me by the hand. I darted furtive glances around me, as though I had found myself there accidentally.

'I'm going back. I've had enough. I can't stay here any longer. I don't want to know what happened any longer, I don't want the flat, I don't want anything from this darkness. I want to go.'

She no longer needed to hear about my new information.

'Come with me. You'd like it. We'll watch films, play on the PlayStation, we can go to concerts... Hangout, maybe have fun... Then we'll see what happens. Whatever happens, anything is better than this here.'

She could see that I was confused...

'I need you...'

It was nice to listen to such an offer, but still I said, 'I can't; you know, I do have a life. I can't just leave everything.'

It was a cynical response and I apologise for that.

She caught her breath.

'As you wish. I have to go. I don't know why, but ever since I came here, I've been afraid all the time. Of everything. All sorts of terrors have returned to me.'

'How many are there?'

'Is that important?'

Both you and I know that that is an extremely important detail.

She said she was sorry she had shouted at me, that she had been nervous, under terrible pressure, and she uttered more, similar excuses. I calmed her down, assured her I was not angry, that that it could happen to anyone... What was I supposed to say? Yes, she had disappointed me, I had put a lot of hope into her, even thought she could save my life. But since then, in a short time, everything had changed. Besides, I have my pride, even though I conceal it skilfully. I imagined that now we had explained everything nicely, at least we could say goodbye nicely. There was no reason for discussion. But, she wanted to talk...

She told me it had been terrible for her since her mother died and she had been left quite alone. She leant on the banister. We fell silent. In order to lessen the discomfort (I don't know why I think I am always the one who has to do that), I asked her how she had found Aleksa's notebook. She said it was waiting for her in the library on the island of Bornholm, on the shelf set aside for the new citizens from Bosnia-Herzegovina. It was peeping out from between Noel Malcolm's *Bosnia: A Short History* and Živko M. Bojanić's biography of Toma Zdravković. She asked me if I could imagine the shock she felt at finding it there? I could, of course. There is nothing I cannot imagine.

So we sat for a time in silence. It was embarrassing, but I didn't know how to start a conversation again. There was nothing to say.

She kissed me when we said goodbye. She kept her lips on my cheek for a few seconds. Until there were goosebumps on my skin. And then she left. I knew, and believe me I know it now too, that I saw her then for the last time.[27]

I had been alone for so long, and then all at once, the same day or evening, I really don't know any more, as soon as Mirna had gone, I had another visitor. Completely unwelcome.

I heard the door of the apartment opening, presumably I had not locked it, even though I think I did and... they were inside. In black suits and with fiery heads. The Pegases. Behind them they left clear imprints of muddy shoes. They paid no attention to me. Albin sat in the chair, turned the television on, turned up the sound and immediately concentrated on a programme about tantric sex. I heard a male voice from the television saying: 'The most important thing of all is that I do not scatter my sperm.' Aldin was examining the books on the shelf. He turned around, looked at me, then at his brother, and coughed. At this, Albin immediately lowered the sound.

'You seem to be waiting for someone?'

I was furious; shaking on the chair.

'Why do you do that? Why do you play with people?'

'Some rule with kindness, your body and life; I shall rule

with the chill of horror,' Aldin recited, while Albin watched him lovingly.

'What do you want with me? Leave me alone!'

Quite calmly he answered, 'We're philanthropists. There is no better way to be aware of the existence of other people than to get to know them completely. That is possible only if you insinuate yourself into their everyday life. Unnoticed... And such a thing, again, is not possible unless you have control over their lives.'

Again he examined me as though I were an interesting object, covered in dust.

'I don't understand why that worries you. That way you are never alone. Only religion can bring such solace.'

Albin added, 'Of course, we need to add that all that has its financial side too. Modern economics seeks complete control of the market. We are, at the end of the day, businessmen after all. Above all else...'

Aldin nodded his head with approval.

'And, in business, discretion is important.'

The last words were directed at me. That was not hard to conclude, because Aldin came right into my face, our noses almost touching.

Albin slipped between us and put his big arms around us.

'Aren't you going to offer us coffee?'

I wasn't sure if I had any coffee in the house at all, but I turned towards the shelf.

'Aren't you going to ask us how we drink it?'

I asked.

'Black as midnight in a night with no moon,' Albin pronounced, and then they both laughed like two squeaking children's toys.

'That's from the television, Agent Cooper, remember?' Albin informed me when he saw that I was not taking part in their enthusiasm.

'Let it go, it doesn't matter, you can see we're not welcome here. Let's go, the taxi is waiting,' said Aldin.

'Is that the good Ekrem?' his brother asked.

And Aldin, looking at me knowingly, confirmed it.

'Who else? Our old war comrade, comrade in arms from the Music School.'

The eerie theatre dolls again threw back their heads in a hissing laugh.

I could take no more, I had to beg them...

'Please, I won't say anything to anyone, just don't touch her,' I squeaked.

'Who?' asked Aldin.

'Romana,' I whispered.

'What's this about Romana?' Aldin asked again.

'The one from the song,' said Albin.

'Ahh, that one,' Aldin remembered.

And they both became momentarily quiet and nodded their heads at one another, as though remembering the verses and melody.

'Do you know where she is?' I asked, in the most polite and most humble tone of voice I could find within myself.

When they laughed, their spittle sprayed on the walls.

'Come with us.'

* * *

On a school trip in primary school, I visited the concentration camp at Jasenovac. After bumping up and down all day in the bus, they showed us a documentary film. We stared at the screen; in the thick silence, no-one dared even to whisper. On the screen there were changing views of massacred bodies, a heap of teeth, a pile of hair, knives for slitting throats, hammers, pits full of bodies. We were about ten years old, maybe less. I was shaking when we came out of the theatre. Then we all stood in a field, in the sunshine; it was unbelievably green, like Teletubbyland. I walked carefully, afraid the ground would open under my trainers and that I would fall into a dark pit full of interwoven, grey, naked bodies, moving in a death rattle and tearing their throats with their nails.

I felt the same thing when I stood on the former open cut, which the town authorities had turned into a rubbish dump after the war.[28] Everything was covered with snow, the rubbish dump was a white field, full of hills. The ground was moving underfoot. If then in Jasenovac I only suspected, now I could be certain, that the ground was indeed gently moving, that there was something alive beneath us... Under the white snow rottenness was seething, feeding the insects, vermin, worms, small creeping things... The whole town's rubbish. Everything people believe they no longer need. What disturbs their lives. What suffocates them. What they can no longer use. Everything they cannot take with them. Everything that brings back bad memories. Something that once was beautiful and no longer is, for which there is no longer any use. Objects which could still be used, but are no longer in fashion. With time they had fermented, lost their shape, colour, original purpose.[29] They had melted into a sludge and become one with the earth.[30] On which the Pegasus brothers and I were standing.

'Aleksa should be here somewhere,' Aldin told me, smiling apologetically and shrugging his narrow shoulders.

'You killed him.'

They laughed, and Aldin retorted in a quite merry voice, 'Don't be a fool. The two of us didn't kill anyone in the whole war. There was no reason for it. There were plenty of people around us who wanted to finally try that out. Probably they thought it was senseless to live to see the war, and not to take anyone's life. We didn't have to tire ourselves, we didn't kill anyone. We encouraged people just by being here. We didn't have to put ourselves out very much. People showed an unbelievable wealth of imagination. They stole the humanitarian aid, and then in the flour and powdered milk they put plaster of Paris to make it heavier, and sold it all on the marketplace. We told you already, we were just the inspiration.'

Satisfied, they looked at one another, they liked that word.

'So who did it?'

'A misunderstanding, that's who. I remember, I told people

to take Aleksa and show him the mine, and they understood....
Fuck, it was war, that's how it was done.'

Then I realised. Horror... Some little, obedient killers had
thought their masters had ordered them to take Aleksa to the
mine and liquidate him there.

'Do you like this explanation? Is it easier now for you to
understand?'

Obligingly the Pegases asked, and looked at the tops of their
shoes. Underneath which, somewhere in the darkness, lay
Aleksandar Ranković, unneeded and forgotten, fused with the
rubbish. Nausea formed in my stomach and rose to my head. I
vomited in strong gushes and drilled orange holes in the snow.
My legs were shaking when the gushing dried up. I sat down in
the snow, in the vomit, in front of the legs of the awful brothers.
Their red heads were burning in the darkness on the rubbish
tip.

* * *

Darkness closed my eyes. It came in the guise of ribbons of
curtains, which became thicker and thicker. Then everything
became quiet. More exactly, some sort of low noise was surrounding
me, like that from a tape recorder. I thought I was sitting on a
small stone floating through space. Completely alone. Yet it was
not unpleasant, I thought I had come like that to the very end, to
the place where I did not have to explain myself to anyone any
more, where no-one any longer expected anything from me.[31]

The calm lasted only a very short time. In one moment, it
transformed into anguish, juicy and strong, probably the greatest
anguish possible: suicidal. There was no way of lessening it,
nothing that could soothe it... All that was left was the firm
knowledge that in this world everything, absolutely everything,
is completely meaningless.

The darkness around me could have been anything at all. It
could have been an opening, a tunnel or a hole through which
ancient beings come into this world.

The earth shook from the stamping of horses' hooves. The darkness swayed. I heard neighing, air hissing through enlarged nostrils. The horses were getting closer, fast, very fast. There must have been a big herd of at least fifty large animals. Fear caused tension even in the smallest vein in my body. I didn't even try to escape, but pulled my head into my shoulders and waited for them to trample me down. Then, all at once, the stamping ceased, as though a huge hand had shaken the horses off the planet.

A light shone through the darkness, lighting up the palms of my hands before anything else. On the far side of the rubbish tip, I saw a completely round circle of light, like a spotlight for cabaret. I was experiencing the same scene that Aleksa had seen, witnessing the same things, which I now I have to describe in the same way. Perkman was coming, the spirit of the pit, the djinn, the gnome, the apparition... A being from the depths of the earth, who appears only to the person who has touched the bottom of his soul. The ghost who saves and warns.

In the middle of the light stood a tall, lean man, dressed in a trailing green coat, with a big round collar and black buttons as big as a miner's fist. He had short, stiff hair, completely white and shining like a neon light. A pale face, narrow nose, eyes without any whites. All exactly the way Aleksa had described, except that this one had a thick moustache. He bowed to me; his body broke in two at the height of his chest. Up until this point I could use Aleksa's precise description, but from the end of this sentence the analogy became absurd. The spirit was known to me, very well known. I stared at him, nervously, slightly apprehensive that the feeling of having already seen him would slip away from me. He smiled and held out his right hand. Then I understood. This was the one thing that was perfectly clear to me... In the familiar, radio-host voice, which the whole town loved, Perkman said: 'Gluck auf'. The greeting echoed across the entirety of the rubbish tip. Every living thing must have heard it. He looked curiously at me, leant his head on his shoulder and waited. It was my turn to speak, yet I didn't know what to say. I couldn't think of anything. I just looked at him and tried to memorize the scene before me. I wanted him to stay engraved in my memory, so I wouldn't forget one detail: the movement, smell, the way the air moved, how the darkness behaved... I must have been completely numb. my face devoid of colour and my eyes wide open, for this is how we usually meet spirits. He studied me, somehow calmly, ready for anything I could say or do. I felt that he felt great empathy for me, an understanding like a pure ocean of pure goodness. That he was the only ally I had in my life. The only support in the darkness.

That darkness around us was not the usual lack of a light source, it was a special world, indescribably rich and full... Yet I felt that my body did not belong there, that my senses did not function there. Aleksa was perfectly integrated into the movements of darkness, he stood squarely on nothing. His presence calmed me; I slowly twisted, I caught the rhythm of breath, I made my own place in that world... Until I began to feel comfortable. Somehow I knew nothing bad could happen to me there. Despite the fact that I had so many things to tell him, I didn't want to disrupt the moment; I wanted again, at least for a little while, to feel tranquillity.

I cannot tell how much time had passed, but it seemed that very quickly he nodded his head and gave me a Valium smile. He said nothing; but I was sure he wanted to tell me how we would meet again. Somewhere, where we could again get to know one another in peace. Now when I think about it, I should have been overcome by despair when I realised he was leaving me, yet I wasn't... I was sure that I would see him again, just as I know that now.

His light filled with red colour, paled and disappeared. We parted. Darkness again took hold of me: normal darkness, earthly.

I had no idea when the Pegases had left the rubbish tip, or whether they saw Aleksa. Except for me, there was no other human presence on the tip. It was only then, left alone, that I realised I was shivering with the cold. Only then that I felt the chill wind chasing across the field.

There seemed no other place to go than back to the apartment, to the place where it had all begun; to the middle of loneliness, in the nursery-garden of fears. I asked myself if the apartment actually existed any more, or if the darkness hadn't gobbled it up completely. Either way, a long walk was ahead of me. Everything would be easier when I stood on firm ground, I hoped.

Who stole from the night the blackest colour and pressed it into your eyes and gave them lustre?

I have no idea how I got home. I dragged myself to the chair, sat down, and felt an unusual coldness. It came from the bedroom. I opened the door with difficulty, as it was resisting. A current of strong fear shook me when I saw that the crack had grown monstrously, devouring a third of the wall. It was impenetrably dark, with a strong wind which seemed to be rushing from an unreasonably large area. I quickly shut the door and pushed my shoe rack up against it.

I was afraid the crack would knock down my wretched barricade, break down the door and get out. Huge and hungry. Perhaps the Big Bang had unfolded into my apartment, but what could a man do with a problem like that? Inform the authorities? Alert Civil Defence that nothingness was threatening to swallow the town? Or maybe I should call Ušušur, the Protector Elf?[32]

When I see Aleksa again, I shall ask him if there is any way I could help him. Was it actually important to him to be buried with some kind of ritual? Perhaps that is an over-appreciated thing in this world? Perhaps our death ceremonies mean absolutely nothing to the departed, and even less to spirits? Perhaps it isn't even that important to them that they have their own piece of land, with a fence, some flowers and a little bench? If there is life after death, what do we care what sort of hole they bury us in? Is it really important to us, while the worms are eating our hearts, whether there are flowers above us?

Do spirits want people to help them at all? I had never heard of somebody helping a spirit, mainly it is spirits who address people... Perhaps it's better being a spirit than being human. Being a spirit has its advantages... You talk when you want to talk and in the way you want to. The people you decide to show yourself to, view you quite seriously, there is no fucking around. You're dead, you're not on this world, but you're still connected to it, you have never really left it.

On the other hand, when you're a spirit, you stay active, you're deprived of the rest you deserve. You are denied the benefits of life after death which are written in the Holy Book.

* * *

Here is the first good news.

The sky finally broke apart and allowed the sun to come out. I didn't manage to see that happen, because I finally slept last night. After I don't know how many days. Under the dining-room table. Fast asleep, without any dreams. If I did have any dreams, I was lucky enough to have forgotten them. To return to that morning: when I opened my eyes, the sun had already entered the room and sucked the damp right out of it. The snow melted quickly, so you could even see with the naked eye how the layer was thinning out. Streams were running down the street, roaring and gurgling, meeting at the marketplaces and forming little whirlpools and waterfalls topped with a dirty scum made up of the filth that had been peeling from the town for days.

And then I saw them...

The terrors! And I learnt something about them that you may not have known: when they are separated from people, terrors look like wreaths, woven out of thorns, teeth, and dirty nails. The water was carrying them. Little ones buzzing like mosquitoes, and heavy ones wallowing like lava or a river of tar. They are as fast as trained dogs when they grab someone's throat, those toothy ones that bite the nape of the neck, the treacherous ones which knock the air out of stomachs, the icy ones that make hoar frost grow on bones... They are unimaginably many, it is impossible to imagine them, even to predict them. Many, many terrors...33 I watched them floating in the immense torrent, swaying with menace, but still obediently following the waves. They were leaving... I would have liked to hear some beautiful music then, so that my pleasure could be complete.

A hand fell down onto my shoulder. Small, narrow, it reminded me of the little hand I had seen on the cover of a Dead Kennedys album. I turned around and saw Aldin. He looked different from usual. His hair was held in place with gel, he wore a metallic grey suit and shoes with a bent tip. That is how the local businessmen – read war profiteers – dress up for trade fairs or religious processions. He was serious, perhaps even a little formal; frowning, coughing a bit and pulling at the lapels of his jacket. His rather strange demeanour made me stand up alongside him, to get myself into the role. We stood facing one another, looked each other in the eye, and yet I managed to calmly endure this encounter with those predatory pupils. Slowly, the blue eyelids slid over them and Aldin, through his sharp teeth, offered me that which cannot be refused. Something which a person whose loneliness has caused him to lose the shape, borders, figure and colour of reality cannot refuse. I accepted and did not ask the price. Apparently, the samurai used to believe a decision should be made only after seven sighs. I did not wait that long.

It was as if we almost hugged at the door. When I closed it behind me, I realised I was completely wet. The sleeves of my jumper had been stretched by so much sweat. But it was not the sweat which breaks out through fear. Because, quite peacefully I heard the cosmos pulsating behind my bedroom door. It was the reaction of my organism to the fact that I could save my life. All I needed to do was to wait for three days.

It was at that point that I decided to write everything down. I wrote without pause, for two days and two nights.

I don't want to forget even one detail, because I feel that each part is important for the whole. I have included unfounded suspicions, unfinished happenings, all those things I cannot explain to myself, nor do I know what purpose they serve... I don't know what's important, and what isn't, because I neither created the story nor can I influence it. I think that it had been waiting for me for years, completely formed and clear. That it had been floating in some place, where the files of events are kept, where they make up the directories of fate, and that in that secret warehouse it was vibrating with impatience for me to set it free. When I finally activated it (through who knows what involuntary action), it completely surrendered itself, it let me peel off its packaging. I feel all the incidents are tied tightly together, that the parts I do not understand are gesticulating around me and waiting to be tied in. I am frightened by the thought that it depends solely on me whether this story will stay tied up or whether it will be unfinished forever, through laziness, ignorance or cowardice, and that with time it will close again. But maybe, I console myself, it will wait for someone else to complete it...

I was writing for that other person. For my unknown reader, be it man or woman. I am sure I do have a reader, because everything written must be read, every sentence is formed in order to seduce the reader, not one letter in the whole world is written for any other reason. I hope my readers will be well-meaning and that my notes will help them. I have bound the pages together, wanting to preserve Aleksa's notebook and his original handwriting. Perhaps in the notebook, the page numbers, or the scratches on the cover there is something I have missed. Maybe some detail of Aleksa's handwriting uncovers more than I have discovered. I am not afraid that I am paranoid. Actually, I am paranoid to such an extent that I don't believe in paranoia.

I did everything carefully, I hope that can be seen. All for that other person. It will be easier for him than for me, if he can endure until the end. I was as careful as I possibly could be, to interest him and thus urge him not to give up and to finish reading the story to the end.

While I am writing this, I don't know what more can happen.

I know I am not the hero of this story, its all-knowing narrator. That one has still to come.

And here I am now. Waiting. I no longer feel any terror. Not even the least of them. On the dawn of the third day, like a self confident despot, I am sitting in my favourite chair. The Irish believe that a house symbolises the emplacement of a man against the unlimited power of the other world. For me, that is what my chair is for.

While the silence pulses calmly, like my heart, I delight in the rhythm of the steps coming closer to my door.

ENDNOTES

1 When I read the description of a room, it is not enough for me to know what the furniture is like, the colour of the curtains at the windows, whether there is fresh fruit in a bowl, whether the walls are decorated with oils or watercolours, whether the table is round or square, in which corner the bookcase is to be found, and where the heater is... I want to be told what sort of music is playing on the radio, or at least what sounds come in from the street.

2 I feel silly for giving up on my own demands, but as you will see, that won't be the first time, I can't boast of being consistent.

3 At that time my wife used to wear her hair up a bun.

4 Paracelsus studied the apparitions of elementals, but also the ways in which mermaids and mermen were formed. He wrote of his visits to mines from Lapland to Ethiopia, from Salamanca to Moscow, where he was a guest of the Russian Tsar. He travelled with a group of Gypsies through Hungary and visited Sinj in Croatia. He tried to make a magic mirror – composed of seven metals, fused into 'electron', a metal only to be found in Hell. Paracelsus believed that only with the help of this metal could one pronounce an exact diagnosis for every illness, because the mirror showed each patient, their illness and the remedy.

5 Mark Twain visited a hospital for the dead in Munich, whose clients were people who during their lives had been afraid they would be buried alive. In the hospital wards, he found bodies with bells attached to their toes. In front of the door stood nurses, listening for the slightest sound from any 'patient'.

6 The feeling of being invisible came to me for the first time while I was doing my National Service in the Yugoslav

National Army. Anyone who has completed this service, which is an excellent name for this obligation, knows how impatiently the recruits await their first outing into the town; how much they want to see again the until then unnoticed charms of civilian life, to feel the air of freedom, to look at people who are free; note details of their clothes, the patterns on the curtains at the windows, the luxury goods on display in the shops; to choose for themselves whether they will turn left, right or round in a circle. But their biggest desire is to see the opposite sex. I remember how sad it made me feel when the girls did not notice me, even though I had cleaned my uniform properly and tightened my belt. They didn't see me even when I stood in front of them. That uniform completely hid me, like Frodo's cloak in *The Lord of the Rings*.

7 She did not leave, she left me. That's how I thought then and how I think now. She began a completely new life, in other rooms with unknown furniture. I remained in the same place, to continually meet with the emptiness she left behind. I am solitary and depressed. A man with no-one to look after him.

8 Later, I read that Hitler also used similar tactics to conquer the masses. I shall transcribe his theory for you, as recorded by Glenn B. Infield:

> Did you know that the circus audience is actually just like a woman? Anybody that fails to understand that the masses have, in essence, a woman's character, will ever become a good speaker. Ask yourselves: What do women expect from men? Clarity, decisiveness, strength and action. What we want is for the masses to go into action. As with women, the masses move between extremes. Crowds are not only like women, but women also make up the most important element in any audience. The women usually lead, then come the children and at the end, when I have won over the whole family, the fathers follow.

9 And what would I do there, in that City of Light, in the Promised Land? Work as a journalist? Maybe my ability to precisely transcribe words directly from the Dictaphone, without thinking about their meaning, could be considered by some an indispensable skill? I began to think about the uselessness of my job for the first time when I was left by myself; in peace, I made an inventory of my life and listed all the absurd things I had to put up with every day. The list was very long. When I finally drew a line under it, I left my job and began living solely from business rental. The rent money is quite enough for me. I have learnt to live within my means.

10 I still wonder what people think of me. Is it possible for someone to be completely indifferent?

11 During the war, I watched some politician visit a unit of the Army of the Republic of Bosnia and Herzegovina. In his honour, in front of the former factory directorate which had been transformed into a headquarters, soldiers were lined up in ceremonial formation. First out of the expensive car were the overweight bodyguards with their walkie-talkies at their ears and their hands on their pistols. Then came the politician in his immaculate suit. A former basketball coach turned brand-new war officer came up to the politician with an amusing marching step, and bawled at him that the soldiers were ready for inspection. The official pulled in his stomach, did up the buttons on his suit, tightened his double chin by lifting his jaw, and like an old penguin waddled in front of the unit. The soldiers lifted their rifles in his honour and followed his comical walk with sullen stares. The politician turned on the heel of his salon shoes, strolled to the middle of the unit on his toes, once more unnecessarily straightened the ends of the fine-quality material of his jacket, became straight as a statue before them and yelled: 'Hail to the homeland!' And the unit in one voice shouted back: 'Hail!!!' The parade was watched by workers whom, for alleged

safety reasons, the police had not allowed to leave the factory. They stood, longing for sleep and their families, at the fence near the factory gates and waited patiently for the comic ritual to end. By contrast with the actors in the ceremony, the workers did not indulge in unnecessary movements. Tired and hungry, they tried to lean against the fence or to sit down on the asphalt.

I don't know even one satisfied worker. I know several people who have become rich since the-war, crazed by unimaginable power, sudden luxury. Almost overnight their lives changed into a cocaine flash. The only thing to be afraid of is that their memories of these days of wildness will pale in their old age.

12 In my town, I know with certainty, everyone has some sort of connection – a family member, cousin, friend, godfather, half-brother, lover or debtor, in some important place. Everyone has someone who can support them, say a good word for them, let them go to the front of the queue. It's strange that any queues exist at all? But, as long as there is still at least one, I am quite sure that I will proudly stand at the end of it.

13 Who was I kidding?

14 Before I went into the gloomy routine of daily newspapers, I had my own music show on the radio. I enjoyed it, I played songs I liked and I didn't care how the listeners reacted to them. I once dedicated a whole program to a girl, as her birthday present. I played only her favourite songs. I remember some of them even now – Lou Reed's 'Sweet Jane', but the Cowboy Junkies version; 'Like a Hurricane' by Neil Young, and 'Fuzzy' by Grant Lee Buffalo; the Tindersticks played the song 'Kathleen' by Townes van Zandt – she liked the part where the strings 'glide' on the recording; 'Famous Blue Raincoat' by Cohen, and Nick Cave sang 'Into My Arms', Tom Waits 'Yesterday Is Here'. But I promised I wouldn't lie. So I will tell you that the girl was my future wife. You could have realised that

yourselves. Why else would I remember these songs for so long?

15 In my opinion this is interesting literature. I appreciate the people who write it and think they shouldn't remain anonymous, because sometimes these little texts are written in a truly masterful way. In three sentences they can summarise the most complicated family drama, historical epic or complex murder mystery.

16 All my life I have avoided obligations, postponing them until the last possible moment. Serious people have no hesitation about how their life should be. They always knew their path, even as children they were gathering their strength. And then with the first signs of maturity they set off into action:

> Education for a lucrative profession – A few experiments with soft drugs, nudism and sex – Employment – A search for the appropriate , healthy, mature and budget-conscious girl – Marriage – Buying a comfortable apartment – Choosing furniture and appliances – Birth of the first child, if possible of the male sex – Buying a car – Birth of the second child, ideally of the female sex, in order to complete the portrait of the ideal family – Building a holiday home – Finding a discreet mistress – Getting a dog, so that the devised family portrait has a more likeable nuance – The fight for the appropriate education for the descendants – Employment for the descendants – Advisory help in choosing their marriage partners – Happiness when the first grandchild comes – Pension – Looking after the grandchildren – Acquisition of a beehive for the holiday home – Preparations for death – Death.

I would need three lives to fulfil this sort of plan. At least. The plan is dynamic, the timetable filled right up, no pauses, no looking back, thereby ensuring that there would be no depression, melancholy. Everything is precise and clean, like a scalpel. Healthy and relentless.

17 They go crazy only when people decide to mess around with their menu. The poor cows, which have always been vegetarian, are pumped up with animal protein in only six months to a size their normal menu would take them two years to reach.

18 Ahmed was quoting the words from a poem by the Portuguese poet Fernando Pessoa. The poet stated that he had ethereal eyesight with which he could see the magnetic aura reflected in a mirror and radiating from his hands in the dark. He related how in one of his best ethereal visions he had seen a man's ribs through his coat and skin and that, at night when he closed his eyes, he saw strange shapes, drawings, symbols and numbers.

He lived in constant fear of madness. He noted:

One of my mental problems – so terrible it can't be described – is fear of madness, which is itself madness.

After Pessoa's death, 25 thousand notes written on little pieces of paper, old envelopes, on the back of letters... were found in a chest.

19 Empty rooms and, inside them, people as alone as fingers. How do we even find one another? Maybe by smell? Maybe we smell of stale air because we seldom leave our hideouts? Or do we know one another by our clothes, by the yellow collars on our shirts? Or by our eyes? By our voice, hoarse from the silence?

20 People are always complaining they have no time. They moan they can't accomplish anything and yet they have at their disposal every possible technical aid for making life easier – cars are faster, plane tickets cheaper than ever before, sneakers have air cushions, with mobile phones and emails all business can be arranged quickly. Yet no-one has any time. Neither do I. Admittedly, I don't have a car, or a mobile telephone, a computer, or even a watch, but I feel as though time is running away from me,

sometimes it seems to me I can see the sun moving across the sky with my naked eye.

21 Once, years ago, I could escape from a dream before it became a nightmare. As soon as I had a presentiment that the dream would change, when I felt that something from its misty edges was beginning to threaten, I escaped. I remember that my escape from sleep was like being covered with wounds. At the top of the dream or on its surface, I don't know what is more precise, some sort of thick membrane was waiting. I pushed my head vigorously through it, the membrane stretched, covered my face and then broke. I awoke with a headache, which hurt the most on the part that had pushed through the membrane. Then, in the apartment with the strange man, I realised that the time for escape had long gone.

22 The editor of *Vogue*, Anna Wintour, has been abusing women for decades. She has a poker player's face and no-one can surmise what she really thinks. But everyone knows she hates women. When she was just 14, she was regularly going for cosmetic treatment and to the hairdresser's, and from early childhood she has chosen her girl friends solely on the basis of the quality and expensiveness of their clothes. Her colleagues in the office say that she is a completely untalented writer, almost half-illiterate, insolent and given to lying, that she takes from people only that which she needs and throws them away when she feels they are no longer necessary. Like every dictator... Environmentalists are in despair at the continual promotion of fur in *Vogue*. As a sign of protest, they threw a dead raccoon on her table in a restaurant. But the cruel ruler of women just covered the body with her serviette and ordered another espresso.

The women who have been buying *Vogue* for years support her tyranny. Maybe they believe that only cruelty like hers can maintain a powerful empire. And the survival of *Vogue* must not be compromised, because only it can offer its followers the hope that with the help of careful combinations of objects of clothing can they find in themselves the strength to feel superior to others.

23 'The consonant "aleph" begins the Old Testament in the Hebrew text of the Bible. In Hebrew it is simply the position of the throat before a sound is made, when a word begins with a vowel. Aleph is, therefore, in some ways the element from which every articulated sound begins, and the Cabalists understood it as the spiritual root of all the other letters, including in its essence the whole alphabet and, with that, all the elements of human speech. To hear aleph, actually, means less than nothing, because it represents the transition towards all possible languages...' (Gershom Sholem, *The Kabbala and its Symbolism*)

24 For her sake, not mine, I shall avoid details. I know she would be horrified if someone were to read our greatest secrets. I have gone a bit too far already with what I have written. Maybe later, when I have more time, I shall wipe from the text those details which are not essential for understanding the story. Right now, I have neither the time nor the strength for that.

25 If the sun was extinguished, the Earth would only live for another eight minutes. I read a story about a young man who carefully thought about what he would do with every particle of every second of those eight minutes. One of the steps to be taken during his preparations was the creation of a list of eight wishes which he must fulfil, at all cost, before the sun went out.

26 Borges wrote about the monster Aheron in his *Book of Imaginary Beings*. He explains that Aheron is the conception of Hell – an animal residing in animals, and described thus:

> That thing is bigger than a mountain. His eyes spark and his mouth is so big that nine thousand people could stand inside it. Two lost souls hold it open just like in Atlantis; one of them is standing on his legs, the other on his head.

Emanuel Swedenborg wrote:

> It is not given to me to observe the general shape of Hell,
> but I have been told that, just like the sky has the shape of a
> man, in the same way Hell has the shape of the Devil.

27 I am sorry I feel like this. It would be nice if I could count
on Mirna as my 'golden reserve'. Because something tells
me I could get used to life in Sweden. There are many
lonely people there. Yet they do not kill themselves because
of that. They go to social clubs, drink on boats, make theme
parties. Alcohol is expensive, that's true, but anyway I
believe there is something seriously wrong with countries
in which alcohol is cheap.

28 Danilo Kiš put it nicely:

> A rubbish bin, like a cemetery, is like a big warehouse of the
> world, the essence. Placing objects one next to another mixes
> the unusual and the miraculous.

29 And everything that loneliness makes of reality.

30 Nature knows not extermination; it knows only transformation. Everything that science taught me, and still teaches
me, strengthens my belief in our spiritual existence after
death.

Wernher von Braun, Hitler's scientist and inventor of the
V-2 rocket, concluded this at the end of his life. After the
fall of Berlin, American soldiers took him prisoner and
conveyed him to the USA. During the Nixon administration,
he worked at NASA. He was a member of the team of
scientists who took the first people to the moon.

Braun's conclusion was used by Thomas Pynchon as
the motto for his book *Gravity's Rainbow*.

31 In my most pathetic moments I thought it would be good
to be an invalid, not too badly mutilated, let's say with one

leg missing... Invalids are treated like people from whom no-one expects anything very important. No-one expects them to be a support, to take care of someone or something. They have complete freedom and can comfortably dedicate their time only to themselves, without anyone accusing them of egoism.

I don't think about this all the time, only when I feel especially unhappy...

32 Ušušur, the green elf, is the protector of the tongue-tied, the melancholy and the mad. An old Slavonian legend says that this elf fell in love with a beautiful girl. When she married, Ušušur put a spell on her and the unfortunate girl drowned herself in the river. The elf was remorseful and jumped into the water after her. To punish himself, he chained his leg to the bottom of the river. In autumn, when the river swells because of rain, he swims up from the bottom and calls out three times: Ušur, Ušur, Ušur! Whoever hears him will die that same autumn. It is believed that Ušušur sits at the bottom of a river in Bosanska Posavina.

33 The worse terror, greater even than the fear of death, is the fear of the future. In our town it is so great that people would rather stay in the same day forever.

NOTES

written on pieces of paper with differing original purposes,
some on pieces of cardboard biscuit boxes, glued on, affixed
with paper clips or just thrown between pages

Cynicism, irony and sarcasm: What are they in aid of? Who needs them? What use are they? Who invents them?

Answer: Nothing; no-one; none; fuck him!

Those who use cynicism, sarcasm and irony think that just because of that they are smarter than their victims. Cynicism, sarcasm and irony are a necessity to liars, smart-arses, fraudsters, perverts, egoists, columnists, humorists, and similar evil people.

How to imprison a spirit:

The magicians of the old Orient could imprison a spirit in a bottle. In a bottle made of brass they put a cat's tail and a few drops of a blue colour. After a certain time, they took the tail out of the bottle and then they repeated 33times the sentence: In the name of Solomon, son of David, prince of magicians, I order the spirit (and they say his name) to go into this bottle. The spirit then appeared and begged the magician to let him go home. But, the reprobate relentlessly uttered: Peace be with you and know, spirit, that your home is now in this bottle and that I am your Master and everything I say to you or do to you will be in your interests and with the aim of helping you. The poor spirit was then transformed into a white cloud and obediently went into the bottle. The magician then put a lead stopper in the neck of the bottle and over it poured hot tar mixed with the sap of the cedar tree.

'The Gift'
(Czesław Miłosz)

A day so happy.

Fog lifted early. I worked in the garden.

Hummingbirds were stopping over the honeysuckle flowers.

There was no thing on earth I wanted to possess.

I knew no one worth my envying him.
Whatever evil I had suffered, I forgot.
To think that once I was the same man did not embarrass me.
In my body I felt no pain.
When straightening up, I saw blue sea and sails.

The poet called this poem 'The Gift'. With good reason. It helped me for years. No longer. I write it down so that someone else may find it useful.

Recipe:
If water were to be poured on the paper on which this poem is written, it would be a fragrant and healing tea.

Calculation:
+6
+9
+200
+0
+6

How metals are formed:
Mircea Eliade researched the beliefs by which springs, mines and caves are identified with the womb of Mother Earth. According to this belief, all the minerals in the bowels of the earth are embryos which mature to become flawless metals. If minerals were left in the earth to grow undisturbed, after maturing for hundreds of centuries, each one would become gold. The alchemists thought that Nature desires to create only one metal; and that only gold is the child of her wishes, her legal heir, because only the creation of gold represents true creation. A certain G. Bachelard said that we must regard the emergence of imperfect metals just as we would look on the emergence of freaks and monsters which come about only when Nature is disturbed in her actions, when she comes across an obstacle which ties her hands, or interference which stops her behaving in the usual way.

THE SEVEN TERRORS

1. Fear of mirrors
When the world is finally silenced, in the cleft stick between night and morning, while darkness slowly mixes with the light, I am afraid to go up to a mirror. I am not sure what I might then see in it. Now, when I think about it, I think I am most afraid of the possibility that I remain completely the same in my reflection, while the things around me become different.

2. Fear of lonely houses
I am afraid that houses in isolation have succeeded in building their own world, which violates all boundaries and rules.

3. Fear of shameful death
I am not sure if I can properly explain this fear, because the boundaries of shame are written differently for each person. But, let's say, it would indeed be shameful if a big fish ate me and took me to the furthest bay to digest me in peace. Or if I died of explosive diarrhoea at a theatre premiere.

Of course, it would also be terrible to die alone. If my neighbours noticed my disappearance only when worms from my body began to invade their apartments.

4. Fear of enormous things
I once visited a factory where there was a press which weighed several tonnes. I stood beside it, terrified by its dreadful strength. I feel the same type of fear near an open space, in front of the high seas, or a soulless plain... I am frightened, too, by assertions about the infinity of the universe, the theory that before the Big Bang there was neither time nor space, and that the whole world is made up of one-dimensional cords which have only length.

5. Fear of large forests
In deep forests, which have succeeded in avoiding the touch of man, ancient secrets still live, because nature has developed there of its own will. And what hero can know Nature's will?

6. Fear of madness

Although, I try to console myself, when a man goes mad, then he is not conscious that he is behaving differently from other people. In my town, during the war a young woman used to walk about, completely unaccountable for her actions and quite naked. While she slowly walked she looked like a film clip from a nightmare. People called her by the nickname Lepa Brena, 'Beautiful Brena'.

7. Fear of loneliness and darkness

Better to write and describe it like this – fear of loneliness or darkness. It's all the same, they both devour.

THE SPIRITS ARE LONELY

Spirits are solitary. It is very rare to see them in a pair. Because of that they have no descendants. They seldom smile, and when they do, the smile is gruesome and unpleasant. They are interested in art, and because of that they help painters, musicians and writers, and sometimes they approach builders. They are not interested in sport. They don't wear watches or carry umbrellas, but still they are never late and never get wet. Sometimes they seek favours from people. Usually this is to do with revenge, a debt which needs to be paid in blood. They pay for a favour with another favour. Their tracks can be caught in sprinkled flour, and their appearance in a black mirror. Horses can smell them out. (*Unclean Forces*, by Nagib Kurjak. Obrazovanje, Vareš, 1969)

FACTS RELATING TO THE PEGASUS BROTHERS

The Pegasus brothers organised an evacuation from the town during the war.

The Pegasus brothers organised a whole string of unexplained murders.

The Pegasus brothers made a graveyard out of the old, open-cut mine.

The Pegasus brothers oversaw torture at the Music School.

The Pegasus brothers are to blame for the death of Aleksandar Ranković, the radio journalist.

The Pegasus brothers control criminal activity in the town.

The Pegasus brothers control the life of the town.

The Pegasus brothers have polluted the town.

The Pegasus brothers have brought evil into people.

The Pegasus brothers can stop the sun from rising.

The Pegasus brothers are to blame for fulfilling the minor omens of Judgement Day

The Pegasus brothers have neither souls nor eyelashes.

The Pegasus brothers like cynicism, sarcasm and irony.

THE MAGICAL HORSE
ČAL-KUJRUK

The Kyrgyz people esteem the magical horse Čal-Kujruk which runs through both worlds. In one epic poem, it says: I can walk in deep water.

In the same poem the rider is warned thus:

'Your shoulders are wide, but your soul is narrow: you don't think.
What I see, you cannot see, what I know, you do not know,
you are brave but thoughtless.

Čal-Kujruk endures terrible agony in order to cross the borders of two worlds. To strengthen his power, essential for the crossing of the abyss between the dead and the living, he demands his rider cut off with his whip a piece of meat as big as a sheep.

ADVICE

Loneliness is that performer which makes reality ferment, which brings a loss of shape, outline, image and colour
Bruno Schulz

Like dark water lives this man
Nâzım Hikmet

Like a tone started by the press of a key, in me there is more death then life
Witold Gombrowicz

A man is human approximately as much as a hen can fly
Louis-Ferdinand Céline

Adults who enter the world of fairy tales cannot leave it. Did you know that?
Gold Mouth to Corto Maltese

And this also, said Marlow suddenly, has been one of the dark places of the earth
Joseph Conrad

I found the notebook buried in a corner of the library, a place I accidently visited for the first time in my life, even though I go to the library nearly every day. I have nothing better to do. It was not hard to find, a few little movements were enough: changing my usual comings and goings, taking my gaze away from a row of German novels, a movement of my shoulders, half a step backward, just two feet from the corner of the shelf, and I found myself in that neglected part of the library, where the texts about mining and metallurgy had been placed, along with exercise books, mimeographed notes, anthologies of superseded works, disproven scientific theses, monographs of factories long ago destroyed, biographies of humanists from the era of socialism, encyclopaedias of out-of-date technology... Forgotten books such as these, books no-one needed. I don't know how I managed to pull out the little bit of book cover that was sticking out. I also don't know why I took it, hid it under my shirt and carried it out, all sweaty with fear that the librarian would stop me. That notebook is the only thing I have ever stolen in my life. It was an exciting experience.

I read it all in one night. I have never been so excited by any reading material. Have you ever experienced that strange feeling when someone shows you an unknown photograph of yourself? It feels as though you are looking at a stranger; of course, you know that it is you, but you don't feel as though it is.

When I lay down after reading, I think I fell asleep in a few minutes. No more than that. But even that was enough for one small nightmare. I dreamt of a small girl, standing alone in the dark, her blue eyes full of tears. She was constantly turning around, as if she were waiting for someone. And that someone was already very late, so the girl thought the person would never come. Because of that she was afraid and her fear was growing every second.

There has been too much fear. Enough for a hundred lifetimes. In life, everything is somehow reduced to love and fear. There is *nothing outside that. All evil comes from fear, wars wake up out of fear, the evil of war from humiliation, and humiliation is what people who are afraid do to others. I no longer have any reason to be afraid. When a man reaches the bottom, as you may already know, having read about it just as I have, there is no other way than to go back.*

Seven empty pages were left at the end of the notebook. That will be enough room for the story which I wish to relate as best I can.

(SEVEN EMPTY PAGES)